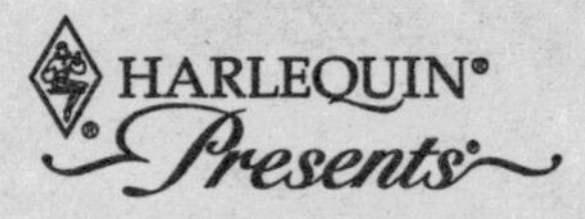

At Harlequin Presents we are always interested in what you, the readers, think about the series. So if you have any thoughts you'd like to share, please join in the discussion of your favorite books at www.iheartpresents.com—created by and for fans of Harlequin Presents!

On the site, find blog entries written by authors and fans, the inside scoop from editors and links to authors and books. Enjoy and share with others the unique world of Presents—we'd love to hear from you!

Relax and enjoy our fabulous series about couples whose passion ends in pregnancies… sometimes unexpected!

Share the surprises, emotions, drama and suspense as our parents-to-be come to terms with the prospect of bringing a new baby into the world. All will discover that the business of making babies brings with it the most special love of all….

Delivered only by Harlequin Presents®.

Sharon Kendrick

ACCIDENTALLY PREGNANT, CONVENIENTLY WED

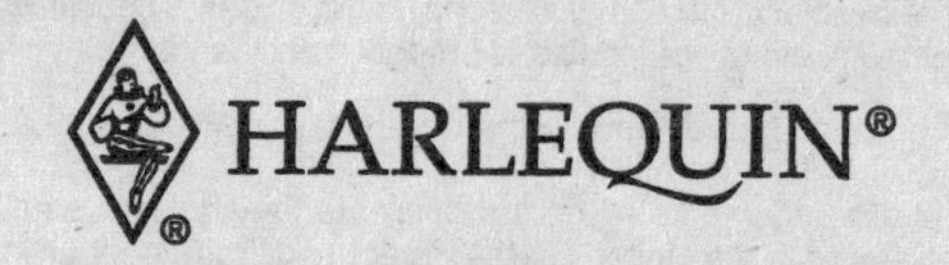

TORONTO • NEW YORK • LONDON
AMSTERDAM • PARIS • SYDNEY • HAMBURG
STOCKHOLM • ATHENS • TOKYO • MILAN • MADRID
PRAGUE • WARSAW • BUDAPEST • AUCKLAND

ISBN-13: 978-0-373-12718-4
ISBN-10: 0-373-12718-9

ACCIDENTALLY PREGNANT, CONVENIENTLY WED

First North American Publication 2008.

This edition published by arrangement with Harlequin Books S.A.

www.eHarlequin.com

Printed in U.S.A.

All about the author...
Sharon Kendrick

When I was told off as a child for making up stories, little did I know that one day I'd earn my living by writing them!

To the horror of my parents, I left school at sixteen and did a bewildering variety of jobs: I was a London DJ (in the now-trendy Primrose Hill!), a decorator and a singer. After that I became a cook, a photographer and eventually a nurse. I was a waitress in the south of France and drove an ambulance in Australia. I saw lots of beautiful sights, but could never settle down. Everywhere I went I felt like a square peg—until one day I started writing again, and then everything just fell into place.

Today I have the best job in the world—writing passionate romances for Harlequin Books. I like writing stories that are sexy and fast paced, yet packed full of emotion—stories that readers will identify with, laugh and cry along with.

My interests are many and varied—chocolate and music, fresh flowers and bubble-baths, films and cooking, and trying to keep my home from looking as if someone's burgled it! Simple pleasures—you can't beat them!

I live in Winchester and regularly visit London and Paris. Oh, and I love hearing from my readers all over the world...so I think it's over to you!

With warmest wishes,

Sharon Kendrick (www.sharonkendrick.com)

To Betty Stephens—passionate lover of life, who has a wicked sense of humor and is a fabulous hostess. And this is a belated birthday present…what a swell party it was!

CHAPTER ONE

SHE didn't want to be here.

Despite the icy blast of the air-conditioning, Aisling could feel a trickle of sweat sliding down between her breasts. But that was the effect he had on her. The effect he had on all women. Some people called it charm, others manipulation. Whatever it was—it was as potent as hell.

'Aisling?'

The richly accented purr of Gianluca Palladio's voice washed into her thoughts like liquid silk, and Aisling composed herself as she turned away from the vast window and its spectacular view of the Roman skyline to the infinitely more distracting sight of the dark-haired man sitting at the desk. The man they called *Il Tigre*—because he was fierce and powerful, and because he hunted alone…

Today his legendary talons were sheathed and Gianluca Palladio looked very much the urban tiger, in a charcoal suit whose dark colour emphasised the impressive breadth of shoulders and the hard, lean body beneath. His shirt was blue—as blue as the bright sky outside the window—and his tie was of gold, as if someone had fashioned it from molten metal and then tied it around his neck where it looked almost dull when compared to the rich olive glow of his skin.

It didn't matter how many times her work brought her into contact with him, it never seemed to destroy the sheer exhilarating pleasure which sizzled through Aisling's body whenever she saw him. But it was a dangerous attraction and Aisling had learnt to suppress it. To present to him the impartial face her job demanded. Doing just that, she curved her lips into a cool smile.

'Yes, Gianluca?'

'You were lost in thought,' he observed softly, his black eyes luminous.

'I was just…admiring the view.'

Gianluca been enjoying his own private view—because Aisling Armstrong's back was far more inviting than her rather intimidating front would suggest. When she leaned forward to peer out at the spectacular panorama like that, then the swell of her bottom brushed against the very uninteresting skirt she was wearing and hinted at the ripeness of the carefully concealed body beneath.

For once she looked almost feminine and soft—an image which was banished when she turned around and presented him with that rather stern and forbidding expression of hers. But then, he wasn't employing her for her decorative qualities, was he?

'It is a wonderful vista, *sì*?' questioned Gianluca softly. 'The best in the world.' His smile was that of a man who was used to only the very best things—who had spent his whole life getting them. Yet Gianluca understood the strange twist in human nature—of not valuing things when they came too easily.

His black eyes flickered to the elaborate white marble construction which rose up behind her, with its row upon row of white marble columns and abundance of statues, and he raised his dark brows in elegant query. 'Perhaps you are taking particular pleasure in looking at the monument of Vittorio Emanuele?' he observed. 'The building which we Romans love to hate and which we call the "Wedding Cake".'

Did his black eyes tease her and his luscious lips caress those last words as if he were eating a morsel of cake himself? Or was it simply that Aisling was a tad sensitive about the subject of marriage, after a summer which had seen her attending three of her friends' weddings. And left her feeling very slightly shell-shocked—as if she'd missed a bus she hadn't even been aware of waiting for.

She looked directly into his eyes, wondering how they managed to be almost soft and yet glitteringly bright at the same time, and then could have kicked herself. Stop it, she thought—with something approaching despair. Stop fantasising about him. Of course his eyes are gorgeous. So is his face. And his body. That rare and interesting smile. Everything about him—even that careless arrogance which he wears like a mantle. And he's a billionaire playboy who's way out of your league in every way that counts—so get real, Aisling.

'I thought that most Romans compared it to a set of false teeth?' she questioned coolly.

Gianluca laughed as he sat back, gesturing to the chair in front of him. He admired her work and—a little reluctantly—he admired her way with words, too.

He had not expected he would employ a woman for such a prestigious role as head-hunter within the hotel arm of his vast organisation, but she had undoubtedly been the best candidate. Yet Aisling Armstrong was the antithesis of everything he sought in a woman.

With her buttoned-up lips and ice-blue eyes—she was so uptight! It was true that her lashes were dark—but did she not realise that a little make-up flattered even the most beautiful of women? Not that anyone would put the icy Ms Armstrong in *that* category. He often wondered why she insisted on concealing her hair like that—yanking it back into such a severe style that it clung to her head like a centurion's helmet. How did you get a woman like this to act like a woman? he found himself wondering.

'You compare this fine monument to a set of false teeth?' he queried, and shook his head, affecting outrage. 'Ah, but I am Italian and I prefer the more romantic version, don't you?'

Aisling didn't react. Given everything she knew about Signor Palladio, she suspected he might be in danger of confusing sex with romance. 'I hadn't really given it a lot of thought.'

'No? Doesn't every woman imagine what her wedding cake might look like, along with what kind of dress she might wear? Is this not the dream which occupies them from childhood?'

She bet they did where he was concerned—no wonder he was so insufferably arrogant. *And so infuriatingly gorgeous.* And wasn't that a big part of what made her feel so uncomfortable—that she, the cautious Aisling Armstrong, should have fallen for a man with such obvious charm?

'Not in this century,' she returned evenly. 'In fact, a lot

of women might be insulted by your assumption that their minds should be focussed on weddings, when there are so many other things to think about.'

'Ah! You are one of these women, perhaps? Do I offend you, Aisling?'

Aisling shook her head. 'Not at all. Feel free to express whatever opinion you like—no matter how outdated it may seem. I can be very tolerant of old-fashioned behaviour—you should know that by now.'

In spite—or perhaps *because*—of her stilted little reply, Gianluca laughed again. In truth, he was bored, and the prospect of some verbal sparring with this woman who always looked like a librarian was enough to whet his jaded palate.

He waved his hand towards the tray of delicious-smelling coffee which one of his assistants had just brought in and placed on the desk. 'You will sit down, and we will take some coffee together.'

'Thank you,' said Aisling, wishing she could get out of it, and that she hadn't given her young assistant the rest of the day off—but if Signor Palladio wished to take coffee with her, then she must comply.

'Now, let me see,' he mused. 'No milk and no sugar, *sì*?'

Aisling raised her eyebrows. 'How amazing that you remembered.'

'Ah, but I remember most things,' he murmured. 'Especially with women who are so secretive about their lives.'

'I can assure you I'm not in the least bit secretive, Gianluca,' she answered evenly. 'I just can't see that it's relevant, that's all.'

He stirred his coffee. 'Don't you know that men are driven crazy by an enigmatic woman?'

'No, I don't.' She took the coffee with a hand she prayed wouldn't tremble, telling herself that he was just trying to wind her up.

Aisling sipped the strong brew. This was the part of the job which never sat well with her. She could do the rest of it standing on her head—all the behind-the-scenes stuff which being a head-hunter entailed.

The quiet searches to find prospective employees. The putting out feelers and all the subsequent interviews to weed out the suitable and the unsuitable. But this bit…the bit that mimicked something social with a man she would never usually have socialised with. A man she found so wretchedly attractive—well, this was much more difficult.

Last night, at the lavish party he'd thrown to celebrate the revamp of his sumptuous new Rome hotel, it had been easy to avoid getting too close to him. He had been surrounded by all the bigwigs and politicians who'd been falling over themselves to speak to the Italian billionaire. As if they were hoping that some of his indefinable stardust might brush off onto them. Stir into the mix the inevitable clutch of beautiful women who were vying for his attention and it was inevitable that Gianluca had been kept occupied all night.

Aisling had spent the evening thanking all those people who had worked away like mad behind the scenes and were often forgotten. Having started that way herself, she identified with them more than anyone—but it was also a good advertisement for her business. She knew that if any of those workers came to England looking for work, then hers would be the name they would remember…

But there was no escaping him today—nowhere to look other than into the ruggedly handsome face and the gleaming ebony eyes which seemed to be silently laughing at her. Sliding into the chair opposite him, she took her coffee and sipped it, remembering the day she'd landed Gianluca's account as if it were yesterday.

Nearly two years ago now—where *did* the time go? It had been her twenty-eighth birthday, which had seemed frighteningly close to the milestone of thirty. And wasn't there something about birthdays which made you look back as well as forward, and regret all the missed opportunities and different doors closed to you for ever?

She had been trying not to think about the fact that she would be celebrating that night with friends who were all in various stages of emotional commitment, and that she had been too busy building up her business to have anything in the way of a love-life. It had come as a shock to her to realise that there was no one in her life who really mattered. Oh, she had plenty of friends, work colleagues and neighbours she knew quite well. But that was it. There was no special *someone*.

She remembered staring at her face in the mirror, searching for imaginary lines and wondering whether she was going to end up as a singleton career-woman—and whether that might not be the best thing. She could think of a lot worse ways to spend your life—and the women she knew who were unencumbered by demanding husbands and equally demanding babies certainly seemed serene enough.

And then she had arrived at the office and there had been a telephone call from one of Gianluca's assistants. It seemed that an existing client had recommended her to the

Italian billionaire and he had a proposal for her—though not the variety which had been so preoccupying her!

Would Aisling like to work for Signor Palladio? To find him a general manager for his brand-new boutique hotel in London? At first she had thought it some elaborate kind of joke because it was the kind of job she'd dreamed of.

The chance of such a lucrative contract would have made the head of any other small firm turn bright green with envy. But she had worked hard for an opportunity like this. Sometimes she never seemed to do anything *but* work, and the Palladio contract had made it all seem worthwhile.

She had told herself she was the luckiest person in the world, but then she had met Gianluca and something inexplicable and unwanted had happened. Her heart had performed a kind of complicated somersault and her legs had turned to cotton wool. Symptoms of love or lust—whichever you wanted to call it—that she'd heard about, but had never experienced before during her erratic history of dating.

And at the same time instinct told her to beware. That the head of the Palladio Corporation spelt *trouble* of a kind which wasn't straightforward. Not simply because Gianluca was impossibly rich and ravishingly good-looking and scarily well-connected and because no sane person ever mixed business with pleasure. But there was something about him which made Aisling feel almost... was *frightened* too strong a word?

It was the way he had of looking at you. Those slanting black eyes lazily scanning every inch of your body as if they had the arrogant right to do so. Putting her in touch with a sensuality she had spent her life repressing—because she knew only too well the risks which sexual hunger represented. Hadn't she seen it firsthand in her mother—the havoc it could wreak?

Aisling knew that Italian men had been brought up to be openly appreciative of women, but when Gianluca did it, he made you feel as if he were stripping you bare with that intense ebony scrutiny.

He was sexy and dangerous. The type of man who collected women like trophies, who enjoyed showing them off and then, when they had lost a little of their shiny-bright newness, discarded them for the next best thing. A wealthier version of the kind of man her mother had been drawn to, and discarded by, over and over again.

And what does his tally of lovers have to do with *you*? mocked a little voice in her head. He certainly isn't known for dating women whose experience with the opposite sex could be written on the back of a postage stamp!

Aisling pinned a polite smile to her lips and tried not to react to the way Gianluca was currently studying her.

'So, Aisling.' He curled the name around his lips as if he were playing with a cherry, prior to biting into it. 'I am pleased. More than pleased. Once again, you have found just what I was looking for.'

'That's the aim.'

'Your initial choice of candidates was a surprise, I admit it,' he conceded, and he raked careless fingers through his thick black hair. 'But, as usual, your favoured applicant was *perfetto*.'

She inclined her head. 'Thank you.'

He frowned. Even in her thanks she was lukewarm! 'You enjoyed the party last night?' he demanded.

'Very much, thank you.'

'I didn't see you leave.'

'I slipped away. You looked like you had your hands full.'

'You should have stayed. There were a few people you could have met. We went out for dinner afterwards—you could have come.'

'That's very sweet of you, Gianluca—but I had some paperwork I needed to do.'

Gianluca's eyes narrowed. He didn't like being described as *sweet*! Sweet was for those men who had manicures and were in touch with their feelings. He thought, not for the first time, how you would never know what was going on her in head—not from that unruffled face she always presented. Was she deliberately mysterious, he wondered, or was that simply a mask she wore for work? And what happened when the mask was removed? 'And business is good?' he enquired softly.

Should she tell him that business was booming? That his name had brought in a whole stack of new contracts? 'Oh, I can't complain. I have plenty to keep me busy,' she said softly, automatically tugging at the dark hem of her neatly tailored skirt, so that it covered the inch of knee it had been revealing.

Gianluca watched the unnecessary movement. The skirt was hardly indecent—didn't she realise that a man liked to look at a woman's legs? She was always like the schoolmarm, he thought impatiently. Even last night she had been wearing some stiff-looking gown—appropriate and yet glaringly dull.

Gianluca had never met a woman like Aisling Armstrong before. Was that why he found her strangely fascinating?

Women rarely intrigued him; their reaction to him was predictable. They wanted him. They wanted his wealth and his lips and his lean, hard body. They wanted a shiny gold band on their finger and they wanted his babies. When Gianluca was around, they pulled out all the stops to make him aware of them, with their tight skirts and their low-cut tops and hair tumbling down over bare shoulders while their lips pouted in provocative invitation. But not this one, it seemed.

'And that is what pleases you?' he mused, meeting her brisk reply with a lazy question in his eyes. 'Mmm? To keep busy all the time? How is it you say—like the hamster on the wheel?'

She wondered if he realised the effect he was having on her—how being in the crossfire of that stare was making her feel as weak as a hamster! Aisling gave him a tight smile. 'It's a question of necessity, Gianluca. I'm sure you know more than anyone that success doesn't come without a price-tag of hard work.'

'Ah, but the trick is in recognising when to take time off, surely?' His eyes narrowed. 'Tell me, when did you last take some time off?'

'I don't really think that's—'

'When?' he persisted.

'I don't remember.'

'You don't remember? Then it has been too long.' Gianluca turned his head to glance out of the floor-to-ceiling windows which filled one end of the large, contemporary office at the top of the magnificent building which was situated right in the heart of the Rome. 'It is such a beautiful day,' he mused, and waved his hand with careless pride.

'See how magnificent the city looks when she is bathed in sunshine. Alive and carefree—like a young girl in love.'

Aisling's expression didn't change. 'Yes. I suppose that's one way of describing it.'

Black brows were elevated. 'You are planning to stay on, perhaps?'

'No. Just until tomorrow. We're flying out first thing.' She wished he would stop looking at her that way—as if she were a specimen in a laboratory that he was just about to dissect.

'Really? That's a pity.' He ran a thoughtful finger over the hard line of his jaw, which already held just a trace of new growth, and stared at her pale face and her set features with something approaching frustration. 'Doesn't Italy tempt you, Aisling?' he demanded. 'Doesn't the successful conclusion of a lucrative contract make you want to take a holiday once in a while—to throw caution to the winds and to drink in the beauty of this country? To celebrate.'

'But I have a business to run. Other clients like you, Gianluca—who'll be wanting my attention.'

'Surely none *quite* like me, *cara*?' he mocked.

To her mortification, his teasing made her composure slip and Aisling felt the hint of colour creep into her cheeks. Some rebel part of her wanted to stand up and say: *There, you've made me blush like a schoolgirl—are you satisfied now?* Except she was certain that she wouldn't be able to cope with his answer.

'No,' she agreed, deadpan. 'Perhaps none *quite* like you.'

His eyes narrowed thoughtfully as he saw the brief rose-pink tinge to her cheeks but he made no comment on it. So she *could* react to a little flirting. Maybe the uptight Aisling

Armstrong wasn't simply the robotic, efficient working machine she appeared to be. 'I can't decide whether or not that's a compliment.'

'Can't you? Well, I know how much you enjoy problem-solving, Gianluca—so I'll leave you to work it out for yourself.'

Gianluca's responding smile was glittering. Ah, *sì*, she was clever—it was why he had employed her in the first place and why her business was doing so well. But wasn't she aware that her frosty attitude was challenging, and that a man with success exuding from every pore of his being found the idea of such a challenge irresistible?

Didn't she realise that if a woman put a wall up, then a man would just want to tear it down with his bare hands? Did he want to do that? He felt the beat of desire as he pushed a plate of tiny *amaretti di saronno* biscuits towards her, but she shook her head. 'What are you doing later?' he asked.

Warning bells rang loud in her ears and, coffee-cup in hand, Aisling stilled. 'Later?'

'Yes, later,' he echoed sardonically. 'Tonight. *When you've finished working*,' he added sarcastically.

'I thought I'd take Jason out for dinner.'

Jason? For a moment, he frowned—until he remembered the gangling male assistant she had brought with her, and made a dismissive little gesture with his hand. 'Why not come to a party with me instead?'

Aisling frowned. 'But we went to a party last night.'

Her obvious disquiet might have amused him for novelty value alone, if the accompanying look of horror on her face hadn't been so insulting! 'That was work,' he murmured. 'Tonight is not. Tonight is for us to be—

carefree...to let your hair down a little.' His glance strayed to the severe hairstyle. 'Literally, perhaps?'

It was an unexpected invitation and for one unscheduled moment Aisling allowed herself the briefest glimpse of a romantic fantasy of imagining just where he might take her and all the delicious possibilities of where such an evening could lead.

Until reality intruded like a cold shower and she put the delicate coffee-cup down with a clatter. 'I can't,' she said unconvincingly. 'This is Jason's first foreign job and I can't leave him on his own.'

'But Jason is a big boy now, *cara*.' His voice became edged with sarcasm, black eyes narrowing like a cat's. 'You can't carry on holding his hand for him for ever.'

'I don't leave my staff out on a limb in a strange city, particularly when they're new,' she said flatly.

'Then bring him along. Come to my vineyard instead.' His mouth relaxed into a hard smile, which didn't quite reach his eyes. A smile which told her that he didn't *do* persuasion. 'It has been the best harvest in a decade and we're going to celebrate.'

For a moment, Aisling couldn't quite take in what he meant. Oh, she knew that he owned a vineyard—he owned two, in fact. But vineyards were rural, and they were slap-bang in the middle of the city. Outside was the busy and bustling *Centro Storico*, and the very nerve-centre of Rome itself.

'I don't think—'

'It will do you good to get out of the city and my country place is only an hour and a half's drive away,' he cut in impatiently. Enough was enough! He was paying her a huge salary and she would damn well do as he wished! Unknotting his gold silk tie, he let it tumble onto the desk where it lay coiled and gleaming like a snake, and his eyes were cold and dark and steady as he fixed her in their gaze. 'I will send one of my drivers to the hotel to collect you,' he stated. 'I would offer to take you myself, but I have business to attend to in Perugia first.'

'I don't have anything to wear,' she said, half to herself. 'Nothing suitable, I mean—and certainly not for a party in a vineyard! I came equipped for business, not parties in vineyards.'

The black eyes flicked over her. *Sì.* He could see that. And suddenly it became an imperative for him to see her dressed up—or, rather, to see her dressed down—to discover whether a real woman existed beneath this cool robot who wheeled and dealed for him. 'You didn't bring any jeans?'

For a *business* trip? Was he out of his mind? To Aisling, jeans reminded her too much of childhood. They symbolised cheap and scruffy, with a lack of formality, which the lonely little girl had longed for. 'No, I didn't bring jeans.'

'Then go shopping. We have some of the best shops in the world right on the doorstep. Buy a pair! *Madonna mia*, Aisling—why do you hesitate? This is an opportunity most women would jump at.'

She opened her mouth to say that she was trying not to behave like *most women*—especially around him. That going to his vineyard was the last thing she wanted.

And yet…

Why had the heavy beat of anticipation begun to slam at her heart? Because this was the stuff of forbidden fantasies she normally only allowed herself on restless nights when sleep refused to come?

It's only a party, she told herself as she nodded, aware of his gaze burning into her as she rose to her feet. But then he turned away and punched out a number on his telephone and began to talk in rapid Italian and she realised he had already forgotten all about her.

And Aisling's fingers were trembling as she opened the office door, wondering why he had issued such an unexpected invitation. To *her*.

An invitation she couldn't refuse.

CHAPTER TWO

'YOU look wonderful, Aisling.'

Aisling forced a smile. 'You don't *have* to say that, Jason.'

'No, I know I don't—but you do! Honestly—you look completely, well…*different*!'

Understatement of the year, thought Aisling as she sat upright against the soft-leather comfort of the car and watched as the lush green hills of Tuscany sped by. She *felt* different, too—and it wasn't just the unaccustomed weight of her heavy dark hair falling about her shoulders or the large silver hoops which dangled from her ears. Nor even the sooty sweep of mascara which made her blue eyes look so enormous.

Where was the cool and calm Aisling she normally liked to present to the world? Gone. That was where. Left behind in some crazy little shop off the Via del Corso!

She turned to look at her strapping assistant who was lolling on the back seat of the fancy car, his legs sprawled out in front of him, as if to the manner born. 'I hope you didn't mind coming all the way out here, Jason—I know I said we'd eat in the city tonight.'

'Mind?' Jason pulled a comical face and gestured to the

picture-postcard countryside which was zooming past the window. 'Are you kidding? I have friends who would die to go to Umbria! To visit a real-live vineyard at the invitation of its world-famous owner!'

In spite of her reservations about the evening ahead, Aisling laughed. As well as tip-top college grades, Jason's enthusiasm was one of the reasons she'd employed him straight after graduating—even though it was sometimes a bit over-the-top. Still, she guessed that was youth for you—and surely it wasn't so long that she'd forgotten her own? 'It's a long way to go for one evening,' she observed.

'In an air-conditioned chauffeur-driven car? Bring it on! Anyway, we've just left the main road, so we must be nearly there.'

Aisling peered out of the window and her heart began to thud. 'So we are.'

It had been an amazing drive. With the backdrop of a big, fat red sun sinking down over the horizon, they had driven past fields full of grazing cows which were the colour of pale fudge. The car had slowed to take in small villages along the way—where the tall, dark spears of cypress-trees made the landscape look so typically Italianate.

Now they were bumping their way up a winding gravel lane which led up a hillside—with row upon row of vines on either side. At the top of the hill was a building lit by the setting sun, so that it looked almost as if it were on fire.

Like a sacrifice, thought Aisling suddenly.

'Hey, it's beautiful,' breathed Jason.

Yes, it *was* beautiful, but Aisling couldn't rid herself of an overwhelming feeling of nerves—and she was terrified that Jason would notice her strange mood and start asking her what was the matter. And how on earth could she put it into words?

Wouldn't it sound ridiculous that the casual clothes she was wearing made her feel somehow *vulnerable*? Like a little girl who had wandered by mistake into the wrong party and wasn't sure just how to behave any more.

She could cope with Gianluca in the relatively safe environment of work, but here, on his luscious estate, with the setting sun making the evening look like the last reel in a corny film—how safe would she be from her own hopeless longings?

As the car grew closer Jason clicked the button so that the electric window slid down and Aisling could hear the sound of music playing and glasses chinking and the rise and fall of laughter and conversation. Driving through an imposing set of electric gates, they drew to a halt in a large courtyard, where a fountain played and a dog jumped to its feet and came running to greet them.

Aisling got out and bent down to stroke the dog, pressing his silky ear between thumb and forefinger, wondering what time she could reasonably slip away, when her thoughts were interrupted by the throaty roar of a powerful engine.

Straightening up, she turned to see a long, low sports car blasting its way up the hillside, spitting up clouds of dust behind it, and Aisling didn't need to see the coal-black hair or lean body to know the identity of the driver. It was evident from that hard, autocratic profile and the tanned forearm which rested on the steering wheel and the sheer, physical presence of the man.

Gianluca turned the engine off, took off his dark glasses and for a moment his eyes deceived him.

'Aisling?' His black eyes narrowed in disbelief. *'Aisling?'*

Aisling wouldn't have been human if she hadn't enjoyed seeing him looking so nonplussed—but the compliment held a sting in its tail. Did she normally look so unremarkable, then? 'Yes, it's me,' she responded coolly. 'Hello, Gianluca.'

Gianluca got out of the car slowly, as if expecting the bright apparition to disappear—like a butterfly suddenly taking flight. He had told her to go shopping and buy herself a pair of jeans, *sì*—but he had not been expecting such a...*transformation* in the process.

Gone was the boring suit and instead she was wearing denim—cut close to the leg and low on the hip and caressing a remarkably pert bottom. Who would have ever believed that her legs would look like that? As if they could go on and on...he swallowed...for ever?

With the jeans she wore some sort of filmy blouse, in swirls of bright, deep colours—hinting at a pair of lush and beautiful breasts beneath. And her hair was down—he'd never seen her wear it like that before. Nor realised it was so thick, or long, or dark.

The tight chignon which usually constrained it was actually hiding a midnight fall of glossy hair which shimmered all the way down to a surprisingly tiny waist. She looked, not exactly beautiful, no, but like someone you would want to explore with your lips and your hands.

'Madonna mia,' he murmured, an unfamiliar note of bemusement creeping into his voice. It was like finding that the onion you were holding in the palm of your hand had

suddenly become the most succulent pomegranate. She was, he realised with a jerk of desire heavy enough to startle even him, the gleaming pearl within the oyster shell.

And despite every instinct in her body telling her not to, Aisling found herself responding to that unmistakable approval on his face, found her body glowing as if it were heated from the hot black fire which was blazing so unexpectedly from his eyes.

Quickly, she glanced over in the direction of the sports car to distract herself. 'That was some entrance you made.'

He studied her, his eyes narrowed. '*Parimenti.* I could say the same about you,' he said drily. 'This is what I believe they call the Cinderella effect, *sì*?'

'Well, hardly. She arrived at the ball in a glass carriage, didn't she? While I've been slumming it in a chauffeur-driven limo,' she said with irony.

He laughed. 'That's not what I meant,' he said softly.

'Isn't it?' Her own voice was equally soft, as if they were sharing some kind of secret. Stop it, she thought. Stop constructing fantasy around an unrealistic desire. Stop *flirting*.

There was a heartbeat of a pause.

'Looks good, doesn't she?' asked Jason chattily, and to Aisling's horror she realised that he might as well have been invisible for all the notice they'd been taking of him.

'Good?' Black eyes were slanted in Jason's direction and Gianluca's mouth hardened. Why didn't this underling disappear instead of making pronouncements on his boss which were inappropriate given his youth and status?

'How you Englishmen are given to understatement!' he said damningly. 'Tonight, Aisling looks nothing less than spectacular. Now come inside and have a drink.'

Aisling felt disoriented—as if she'd just woken up from a long sleep—and it was nothing to do with the car-ride or the warm and balmy evening. Because her host also seemed to have undergone a transformation, she thought—and this was Gianluca looking more approachable than she could have ever imagined.

He, too, was wearing jeans. Faded blue denim which clung lovingly to the hard muscular shafts of his legs in a way that his elegant suits never did. His shirt was made of some fine, silky material and several buttons were open at the neck, so that a dark sprinkle of hair was visible as it tapered downwards. The city-slicker had given way to elemental and earthy man and it was taking some getting used to.

There was something about the way he was looking at her which was different, too—and a million miles away from how he had been in the office earlier. Then he had seemed as if he was trying to tease her into some kind of reaction, but tonight it was as if he wanted…

What?

What do you think he wants, Aisling? she asked herself. A stupidly vulnerable woman all too ready to read something into his actions which he had not intended? What do you think that this stud of an Italian heart-breaker wants from little old *you*?

In the warm Italian night air, she shook her head and felt the shimmer of hair over her bare shoulders as she reasoned with herself. You are going to stop this right now. You are going to take control of yourself and your emotions the way you always do. After all, it wasn't really such a big deal to socialise with someone who employed you. *Unless you let it be.*

'Come now, you must taste my wine,' said Gianluca with a glittering smile.

Aisling began to despair. Did that question sound deliberately erotic, or had her senses just gone haywire in the warm, scented air of the evening? 'That would be wonderful,' she agreed neutrally, as if he had just suggested reading through a stack of dry legal documents.

'And, Jason—it *is* Jason, isn't it?' continued Gianluca softly, with a faint frown. 'You must let me introduce you to some people.'

They walked out to a big, old barn, which seemed to be full of guests—a high, galleried building with tall ceilings and whitewashed walls, oak mangers and stone-paved floors. There was a split-second pause as the three of them walked in. The small band stopped playing and everyone began clapping as Aisling heard Gianluca's name being shouted.

She saw him shake his dark head and say something expressive in Italian and then there was cheering—and the violin player burst into a little jig as he guided them through the hoards who stood to one side to let him pass. Men's hands slapped him on the shoulder—which, to Aisling's surprise, he didn't seem to mind at all.

She could hear *grazie* being said over and over again. 'Thank you?' she translated, on a question.

'They are thanking me for the good harvest!' he laughed. 'As though I am personally responsible for the lack of frost and rain and the long, hot summer in between which has meant that our grapes were as succulent as they could be!'

How relaxed he was, she thought as she looked on the unfamiliar gleam of laughter on his mouth. As if someone had peeled away an urban layer of sophistication to find an earthy man of the land beneath.

Somewhere along the way, he delivered Jason into a group of young people and handed her a glass of wine before introducing her to a dizzying array of people including the estate manager, his old nanny, two godsons and even the local mayor!

It was not what she had been expecting and more than a little intoxicating. The genuine affection with which he was greeted by his estate workers didn't fit with her hard and driven image of him, and Aisling was slightly relieved when someone came to claim him. Much more of this and she would be signing up to his fan-club!

He gave her an expansive shrug before being borne away, leaving her with Fedele, a charming man in his fifties, who was Gianluca's lawyer.

'Well, I am his *local* lawyer,' he emphasised slowly, in perfect though heavily accented English. 'He uses a different one in the city. A specialist for every need at *Il Tigre*'s fingertips.' The lawyer's eyes were curious. 'And you? You are his latest woman, *sì*?'

Aisling found herself blushing. 'Oh, good heavens, no—it's nothing like that!'

Fedele laughed. 'Most women would not find that such a horrifying proposition!'

'I work for him, that's all.'

'Ah! And what do you do?'

'I'm a head-hunter.'

'Cacciatore di teste?' Fedele translated.

Aisling had heard the phrase before and she smiled. 'That's right—somehow it sounds much better in Italian.'

'That is because everything sounds better in Italian!' came a soft, arrogant boast from behind her, and Aisling turned to find Gianluca's mocking black eyes on her. 'And do you know why that is, *cara*?'

Like a snake hypnotised by the charmer's pipe, Aisling found herself shaking her head. 'No. Why?'

'Because we Italians *are* better at everything.'

'That's…outrageous,' she protested.

He shrugged. 'Ah, but it is also true!'

And try as she might—Aisling couldn't do anything to stop smiling or prevent the slow, unfurling of desire in the pit of her stomach. Suddenly, she felt like a non-swimmer who was out of her depth—and that was a very precarious place to be.

'Your glass is empty,' he observed. 'Come, let us find you another drink.'

Had she really drunk a whole glass without noticing?

Gianluca took her to the far end of the room where wine was being served and poured them both a couple of glasses, watching her as he raised his glass. This morning he had idly been wondering whether a real woman lay beneath the outer armour of her unimaginative suit—but the contrast between what she had been and what she had now become was blowing his mind. His senses were shocked and his body was aroused and he wanted her.

Now.

'So,' he said huskily as he touched his glass to hers in a toast. *'Salute.'*

'Salute,' Aisling echoed as she manoeuvred the drink to her lips.

'You like it?' he queried softly.

'It's…wonderful.'

'Ah, Aisling—but you find everything wonderful tonight,' he teased.

'You'd rather I objected?'

His lips curved. 'Now *that* is more like it.'

'Oh? And what's that supposed to mean?'

Gianluca heard the defensiveness in her voice. Did she have an Achilles heel like other mortals? Was the ice-maiden seeking his approval? 'One of the reasons you are so good at your job is because you have a critical and discerning eye—but it seems to be absent tonight. And that is no bad thing.' He smiled. 'Relax, *cara*. Don't look so tense. Tell me what you know about wine.'

'Well, nothing really,' she said quickly. 'Except how to drink it.'

'Then perhaps I should educate you. What do you think—would you like me to teach you everything I know?'

Aisling bit her lip. *Everything he knew.* How much would that be? As she met the sensual question in his eyes she found herself wanting far more than being taught about wine appreciation. Gazing at the perfection of his hard body, she found herself wondering what it must be like to be made love to by him. Had he *meant* her to think that? You *work* for him, she reminded herself—but it didn't seem to alter her chaotic thoughts.

'Education is never wasted,' she said primly.

Gianluca gave a soft, low laugh at the repressive note in her voice and felt the ache in his groin increase. *Ah, sì.* This was novel indeed. A woman who was keeping him guessing about whether she would let him make love to her. 'Then let me be your teacher,' he murmured.

She wanted to tell him not to be so provocative—but what if that was simply her interpretation of his behaviour? A repressed single woman's wildest fantasies. What if he was just being an affable host, out to give her an enjoyable time after the successful completion of a job? Who was to say that he wouldn't have been behaving this way if she had been a man?

But if she'd been a man, surely he wouldn't have been standing quite so close to her, so close that she could smell his subtle scent—evocative of sandalwood and citrus and something else which seemed to symbolise everything that was masculine. From this near she could feel the heat radiating from his powerful frame, and see a tendril of dark hair which curled onto the olive sheen of his skin, so that at that moment she found herself wanting to curl that errant lock around her finger.

'You know how to drink it—to best enjoy it? No? Then I shall show you. First, we look at it.' Gianluca held his wine up, swirling the claret-coloured liquid around the bowl of the glass, so that it left sticky little trickles running down the side. 'See its beauty? Like the richest rubies, *sì*?'

'Y-yes.'

He shot her a look before briefly lowering his nose to inhale deeply, his dark lashes arcing downwards to shield the dancing dark light in his eyes. 'And then we breathe it in. We inhale its bouquet. We engage the senses before at last we feel it on our tongue to taste it, and then, at last, we savour it.' His eyes captured hers over the rim of the glass before taking a slow mouthful of the dark red wine and moving it around his mouth in a gesture which was sheer eroticism.

'You see, the anticipation of pleasure only adds to the

eventual enjoyment—as it does with all the pleasures in life,' he finished and waited for her to bristle with her very English disapproval. But to his surprise, she did no such thing.

'I see,' said Aisling faintly, completely mesmerised by the silken caress of his voice. She wondered what spell he had cast to root her feet to the spot like this, to make her want to carry on looking at that beautiful, rugged face until the end of time. To want to touch her fingertips to its glowing skin and trace the line of those perfect lips.

Oh, Aisling, Aisling, you've started to commit that sad sin of women nearing thirty—who believe that fairy tales really can happen.

At work, she was better equipped to deal with his charisma, yet it was as if by coming here tonight, and putting on these jeans—which were clinging rather suggestively to her bottom—she had removed whatever it was which usually kept her safe. She had put herself at risk, and she needed to do something about it. The question was what.

'You like this wine?' he queried.

'I like it…very much.'

'Perfetto.' He took another sip, aware that his heart was pounding with a strangely slow and heavy beat. He could see the swell of her breasts brushing against the fine material of her top and, despite the warmth of the evening, how her nipples were perking in pert points.

He was aware of the sweet pain of his erection, which was pushing against him, and suddenly he felt like a schoolboy, aware that the evening had cast him into a role in which he was unfamiliar. That for once he was playing a game and he didn't know how it would end—or even which rules to engage. Normally, when he wanted a woman he didn't even have to try. A glance, a murmur, a hint of sensual promise in his eyes was enough to capture his quarry.

Yet with Aisling, it was different. The unthinkable had happened because he simply didn't know whether she would be willing to be seduced. Or whether you should be breaking the rule of a lifetime and sleeping with someone with whom you have a professional relationship—someone you employ!

But he ignored the voice of his conscience—for something much more compelling was driving him. He wanted her and he would have her. 'We should eat something,' he said suddenly.

Aisling looked at the nearby tables, which were completely covered with food. Platters of anchovies and whitebait, and colourful dishes of salad. A whole small roasted pig sat close to pasta with wild boar and truffle sauces and yet another table was stacked with cheeses and figs and ripe peaches, the fruit tumbling over the bowls like a still-life painting.

The whole scene was exquisitely beautiful and yet, more than anything, it seemed to represent the huge differences between them. This was the kind of world Gianluca had grown up in, Aisling realised with a pang. One rich with culture and tradition and wonderful fresh food.

She recalled her own meals of something on toast—meals she'd cobbled together after school—her ear always half cocked for the door, wondering whether her mother would make it home that night.

But there might as well have been sawdust heaped on the table for all the temptation it offered and Aisling had never felt less like eating. 'I'm just not very hungry,' she said weakly. 'It's too hot to eat.'

'Yes. Isn't it?' Much too hot. He felt the flicker of a pulse at his temple because he had seen her watching him and he wanted to kiss her. Instinctively, he knew that this was the moment to strike, when her lips were half parted in that unconscious invitation, when her whole body had softened—her defences down. He felt the slow, irresistible pulsing of desire.

'Why don't we go outside? It will be cooler there and we can look to see if there are any shooting stars. Have you ever seen one before?' Aisling shook her head.

No? But that is an unspeakable crime!' He smiled. 'Don't you know that the Italian skies are full of them?'

And despite the tension which thrummed between them like the heavy, electric atmosphere before a storm, Aisling laughed. 'Oh, really?'

'You don't believe me? Then come and see for yourself.'

It was one of those life-defining moments. The fork-which-lay-in-the-path moment. The tantalising difficulty of deciding which direction to take. Play safe like she always did—or live dangerously? The quicksand gave way beneath her feet. Just this once, she thought...*just this once.*

'Why not?' she said lightly, as if it didn't matter. And it *didn't* matter—at least, not to him.

And to her?

Aisling didn't know. A lifetime of hard work and denial and playing to the rules had been vanquished by the tall, powerful man they called *Il Tigre* on that scented Italian evening. Something alien and tantalising was driving her and she was being propelled by an instinct she was in no mood to fight. Or maybe it would have taken a stronger woman than her to fight the night and the moonlight and the man. *This* man.

Her heart was beating very fast as they stepped out into the scented air and walked away from the noise of the party in silence, like two conspirators.

The moon was full and the sky full of stars but they weren't moving anywhere and Aisling quickly turned her face upwards, as if to reinforce the real reason why they were out here. Except that deep down she knew it was not the real reason. Because who cared about stars?

'Which shooting stars? I can't see any,' she said, in a voice which didn't sound like her own.

'It is a little late in the year,' he conceded, but he wasn't looking at the sky—his attention was captivated by a cloud of dark hair and the pale profile which looked as if it had been carved from marble—intensely beautiful because it was so unexpected. How could he have been so blind not to have seen her loveliness before?

'You see them mostly in August,' he said distractedly. 'The feast day of St Lorenzo is known as the night of the shooting stars—and then you can see meteors showering the skies like fireworks. People consider them lucky and they make a wish.'

'Gosh. How…romantic.'

'You like that?'

'Who wouldn't?'

'And yet this morning you told me you preferred the pragmatic approach,' he mused.

'Did I?' But this morning seemed a lifetime ago. She kept looking upwards towards the heavens, losing her gaze in its star-studded blackness, terrified of what she thought might be about to happen—and yet her heart was beating fast with a mad kind of eagerness because she wanted it to begin.

'Aisling?'

His soft voice made her stop looking at the sky and turn her gaze instead to the sculpted shadows of his face. In the dim light she could see the glitter of his eyes and the gleam of his lips.

Her voice was tremulous. 'What?'

'Do you know what I would wish for, if I saw a star blazing across the night sky right now?'

She shook her head, so that the hair moved like a heavy silken curtain. 'No.'

His lips curved into a mocking smile. 'Yes, you do,' he taunted softly as he pulled her into the shadow of a large tree and into his arms.

CHAPTER THREE

HIS body was hard, his breath was warm as he pulled her close against him and Aisling could scarcely breathe as every longing she'd ever had about him fused into that single moment. 'Gianluca!' she gasped, her voice a mixture of plea and protest.

'*Mia bella!* Kiss me. Just *kiss* me!'

'But this is wrong!'

'Why is it wrong? How *can* it be wrong?' he demanded.

She tried to think of a reason but her brain had gone to mush and so had her body. Was it the raw urgency in his voice which made her want to obey him without question, or her own overwhelming hunger which made Aisling stay right where she was? Perhaps it was simply the fleeting feeling that if she didn't, then she would regret it for the rest of her life. That she would become one of those bitter old women who had rejected a taste of paradise when she'd had it offered to her on a soft, warm night in Umbria.

'You know you want me,' he asserted harshly.

'Yes,' she assented breathlessly. And with a little moan, she wrapped her arms around his neck, lifting her mouth to meet his hard, seeking kiss.

A thousand fireworks exploded in his head as her lips opened beneath his. 'Aisling,' he groaned, her name as unfamiliar on his lips as the taste of her, the smell of her, this sheer unexpected reality of having her soft and compliant and oh-so-hungry in his arms. The ice-queen melting! The cool Englishwoman kissing him!

Aisling swayed as she responded with a fervour which seemed to sap her of strength and reason. His hands were touching her breasts, and—oh, heavens!—she was *letting* them, as if it were the most natural thing in the world. Fingertips moving over her body, as if examining her by touch alone. Lingering at the indentation of her waist. Skating over the curve of her hips. Cupping the swell of her buttocks and pulling her into the hard rock of his arousal.

'Oh!' she gasped.

'You like that?'

'Yes!'

'And that?'

'Oh, yes.' She breathed. *'Yes!'*

'You want me to keep doing it?'

'Yes!'

He flicked his tongue over her bone-dry lips. She was like molten lava, bubbling beneath his touch—so responsive, so unbelievably receptive in a way which belied her normal cool image.

Gianluca thought quickly. If his barn were not filled with villagers and local dignitaries, he would have thought nothing of taking her there, beneath the tree. He could have fought to get her jeans down and thrust deliciously into her. Then they could have gone back to the party afterwards as if nothing had happened.

He frowned with concentration. If he kissed her thoroughly enough, silenced the sounds of her orgasm, he might yet be able to accomplish it. And yet he was still not certain of her. Some women were needlessly sentimental when they took a new lover—insisting on the formality of a bed rather than a shadowed space in an orchard. Would Aisling be one of them?

He realised that this was madness—that there were a million other women more suitable to take to his bed than this one. She was a good head-hunter and this could impact badly on their professional relationship. Yet for once he failed to heed the note of caution in his head. He wanted her in a way which surprised him. Against her lips, he smiled. He wanted her and he knew how to guarantee that she would be his.

He moved his hand to touch her thigh through the thick material of the denim, feeling her shudder against him.

'Gianluca?'

The word came out breathlessly against his lips and he heard her uncertainty. Ruthlessly, he moved his fingertips upwards, alighting and burrowing over her mound with irresistible precision, and heard her helpless little moan.

'You like that too, I think, *cara mia*,' he murmured, and now he began to move his hands with accurate sweetness, knowing that the barrier of her jeans was exciting her as much as frustrating her. 'Don't you?'

The world tipped on its axis as for one second Aisling really thought she was about to lose it there and then.

'Don't you?' he prompted huskily.

Mutely she nodded her head—words beyond her ability as she clung to him with all the hunger of someone who hadn't had sex for so long, she'd almost forgotten what to do. But it was more than that, wasn't it? It was because it was him—her every fantasy personified. 'Gianluca,' she moaned.

'We can't stay here,' he ground out.

Again, it was a statement. He was not given to asking permission, Aisling realised weakly—in the same moment realising that she didn't *want* him to ask. She wanted him to take control in that masterful and autocratic way of his. Because that will take some of the self-recrimination away—is that why? questioned a mocking voice in her head, but she silenced it.

'I know,' she whispered, her answer making her complicit in what they were doing.

Those shaky words were all he needed—and he didn't realise how much he had been fearing that she would tear herself away from him and let sanity prevail until he heard the rush of pent-up air escape from his lips. The slow seep of anticipation began to ensnare him and, compelled by some primitive instinct, Gianluca did what he had never done before. He picked her up in his arms and carried her up towards the house.

'Put me down,' she whispered.

'No.'

'I'm much too heavy.'

'*No*. You are perfect.'

It felt like being in a dream, as if she had spent her whole life waiting for just that moment. Cradled in Gianluca's strong arms with her head resting against his chest in the warmth of the balmy night and a silver moon blazing overhead.

She barely noticed the cool, dim house with its ancient

flagstones and its worn stone steps and beautiful old furniture—all she could feel was the pounding of his heart against her body. Gianluca didn't even put her down once they were inside—instead he began to mount the stairs with Aisling still in his arms. How strong he was, she thought, in admiration and slight bewilderment.

The first moment of panic she knew was when he kicked open a door which revealed a huge bed, its counterpane and cushions covered in some dark, silky material. An unashamedly masculine bed which looked made for seduction—and Aisling suddenly wondered what he would expect of her in return. Would she let herself down with her relative inexperience?

Her tongue snaked out over bone-dry lips. 'Maybe this isn't such a good idea,' she whispered.

He had been expecting this, but it didn't stop him from laying her down on the bed as carefully as if she had been composed entirely of something fragile. He smoothed a stray tendril of hair from her cheek, his black eyes suddenly serious. 'Oh, yes, it is,' he affirmed softly. 'It is the best idea I've ever had.'

And then he bent over her and kissed her with a different kind of kiss from the one beneath the tree—it was all soft and tender and stomach-melting—the kind of kiss which said: *Trust me*. Could she? More importantly, could she trust herself not to read anything more into this than what it really was? If she was prepared to accept reality for just this once, then she would be safe.

Gianluca felt another unexpected kick of something which seemed to exceed mere desire as her arms looped up behind his neck and her lips parted as she stared up at him in silent invitation. Her dark hair was fanned out against the gleaming backdrop of the bed, the filmy top outlining her amazing breasts and her denim-clad legs splayed out in careless abandon.

His lips began to graze over her eyelids. 'Do you know how beautiful you look tonight, *cara*?'

'Seriously?' she questioned uncertainly, guessing that this was what he said to every woman he took to his bed. But it unsettled her. She might have scrubbed up well tonight, but no way was she *beautiful*.

'Oh, yes.' He felt her tense and his hand cupped her breast until he felt her nipple peak against his palm and he wanted to say to her— Why the hell don't you dress like this normally? Except to say that risked bringing work into the bedroom and destroying the enchantment.

So instead, he whispered to her in Italian, telling her that she was much too beautiful to hide her hair and body away—allowing himself the luxury of knowing that she could not understand anything he was saying. So there was no chance his words could be misinterpreted…only their sensual tone would be taken on board.

He felt the apprehension begin to leave her as he told her that her hair was as dark as the night and that she looked like a sorceress. He told her that her body was everything a woman's body should be, and as he tugged off the jeans he realised that he had been right. *Madonna mia*, but she was a Venus! It was true that her lingerie was a little on the plain side, but he wasn't intending that she wear it for very much longer.

'Gianluca,' she breathed as he slid off her panties and tossed them aside to join the other garments on the floor.

And suddenly the uncertainty began to dissolve with the sure caress of his fingers against her nakedness and his murmured words.

He was just so gorgeous, and he was making *her* feel gorgeous—and hadn't she been nurturing a fantasy about this man from the very first moment she'd met him? Reaching up, she burrowed her fingers beneath his silken shirt, feeling the flat, hard planes of his torso and the rough texture of the hair which grew there.

'*Sì*, touch me,' he urged, and closed his eyes as she began to unbuckle his belt, as he had prayed she might. 'Do not be shy, *cara*. Ah, *sì*—touch me right *there*.'

The momentary inhibition Aisling felt at the formidable length of him against her palm was soon banished by the groan of pleasure he made and now she felt powerful. Equal. Because she wanted this, too.

She wanted it enough to forget everything but the potent strength of her own desire, which had her tugging off his jeans and hearing his low laugh until suddenly they were both naked, their bodies and limbs entangling, and Aisling gave a little cry of delight.

Gianluca kissed her and touched her until she cried out for him to take her and that made him laugh and kiss her some more. 'Shall I make you wait?' he teased.

'Don't you dare!'

'Or, what?'

'Or…this…'

She took her hand away from where it had been playing with him and he groaned, even while he wriggled with pleasure. So the cool and contained ice-maiden was melting, was she? Inside she was as hot and as sexy as any woman he'd ever made love to. He moved over her, brushing aside a few wild strands of dark hair, kissing the tip of her nose, and suddenly he was overcome with a need to make love to her.

'Aisling?' he said unsteadily. 'You are protected?'

As Aisling shook her head he groaned and reached for some protection, stroking it on with shaking and impatient fingers and then moving over her once more.

There was that split-second before he entered her which somehow felt as intimate as anything could be. She wanted to tell him that she never normally did this kind of thing, that this was special, but she sensed that it would be inappropriate. As if she was expecting too much from it…

And besides, Gianluca was too aroused to be able to hear anything and so she just drew him down to her, wrapping her arms possessively around his bare back, wanting him closer than close—on her and in her and… 'This is…'

'I know it is,' he groaned as he delayed for one more blissful and agonising second. *'Il settimo cielo.'*

'What does that mean?'

'It means that it feels like heaven. That *you* feel like heaven.' And then he thrust into her—slow and hard and deep—enjoying the cry of delight which was torn from her lips as they moved in the act of life itself.

Again and again, he brought her to the edge—teasing her into writhing submission until suddenly he knew that he could wait no longer. He bent his mouth to her nipple, his teeth grazing against the sensitised bud, so that her nails gripped into the flesh of his shoulders when at last she tumbled over the edge and he winced with the heady combination of pleasure and pain before he climaxed himself.

They lay there, tight together, moist bodies mingling as their breathing and their hearts slowed, and as a delicious torpor began to creep over him he lifted his arm up to glance at his watch and swore very softly.

Sleepily, Aisling lifted her head. 'Is something…wrong?'

He yawned and shrugged. 'I'm not exactly behaving like host of the year, am I?' he murmured. 'We'll stay here for a while, but then we really ought to get back to the party, *cara*.' But the temptation of a goose-down heap of pillows and a warm, naked body next to his was just too much to resist and Gianluca fell asleep—a naked thigh spread carelessly against the curve of her hip, one hand lying lightly just above her waist, a few stray tendrils of hair like silk bonds against his skin.

Aisling must have slept too, because when she awoke she felt both disorientated and yet utterly contented. Her limbs felt heavy and her body warm and replete—its sticky heat and the tingling sensation of her skin reminding her of…of…

Her eyes flew open and she experienced a momentary feeling of sheer, blind panic as she realised just where she was.

And with whom!

She swallowed. It couldn't be. She must have dreamt it. Please may this be a dream.

But then she heard the sound of a small sigh and the stirring of a body beside her and she knew that it was no dream.

Scarcely daring to breathe, she carefully turned her head to look at the figure on the bed next to her, as if seeking visual reassurance that she had really just slept with her client.

In sleep, Gianluca's face was much softer. The ruffled hair and dark sweep of his lashes made him seem a million miles away from the high-powered executive with the restless nature and rather cruel smile. For one mad moment she almost gave into the overwhelming desire to lower her head and to whisper her lips along the olive silk of his bare shoulder and to move her body over his, until a wave of reason washed over her like a cold shower, bringing her to her senses.

In the air was the sense of utter silence which told Aisling that it must now be the middle of the night—and, apart from the dawning realisation of what she had done, something else jarred at her conscience.

Jason!

Aisling froze. She had brought her young assistant to a party in the middle of nowhere and she had disappeared halfway through without a word, in order to sleep with their host!

A tiny moan escaped from her lips before she could stop it and the figure beside her stirred again. Aisling hastily clamped her lips shut. She needed to think. To decide on a plan of action—or rather a damage-limitation plan.

Ruthlessly, she quelled the aching in her heart and the wistful little voice in her head which kept telling her how wonderful it had been. Maybe it had, but it should never have happened—and whether she blamed the wine or the moonlight or her longstanding infatuation with him, none of that mattered. It *had* happened—that was the only thing which counted, and now she had to get out of here. She ran through the options in her mind.

If she waited until morning, then not only would she have the embarrassment of facing Gianluca, but also of facing however many staff he had working here. How the hell would *that* look? She bit her lip as she remembered him introducing her to his old nanny last night and that nice local lawyer. It would look exactly what it was—that she had behaved like a tramp! And then she remembered Gianluca looking at his watch after they'd made love and saying that they really ought to get back to the party.

Now that didn't sound like the behaviour of a man who wanted to eke out every last moment or lie around stroking her face and telling her that it had been wonderful, did it? No, it sounded exactly what it was—that she had presented him with an opportunity for seduction and he had seized it like the red-blooded man he was.

But what did she do now? And where the hell was Jason? Had he taken the chauffeur-driven car back to Rome or was he asleep in one of the bedrooms of this large house?

With all the stealth of a cat-burglar, Aisling wriggled slowly from beneath the muscular body of Gianluca—but he was so deeply asleep that she was able to extricate herself and her clothes and handbag and slip from the room without him waking. She found a bathroom down the corridor and as silently as possible scrambled into her underwear and jeans and tugged on her top. Then she pulled her mobile from her back pocket and found two text messages there from Jason.

'Where are you?' read the first. 'Gone back 2 Rome. C U on flight 2moro?' said the second.

Aisling breathed a sigh of relief. At least Jason wasn't stranded out here as well—which meant that she didn't have to worry about finding him.

The question was how she intended getting back to Rome in order to guarantee catching her early morning flight and putting as much distance between her and

Gianluca as possible. Surely that was the best possible scenario—allowing them both the dignity of pretending it had never happened.

If only she weren't stranded.

But then Aisling remembered Gianluca's entrance in the gleaming sports car and an idea began to slowly grow in her mind. A plan so unlike what the usual cool and careful Aisling would have devised that it made her realise just how much her senses were spinning. But not enough to stop her thinking it through.

What was to stop her borrowing *his* car to get back to Rome? He was bound to have a satellite-navigation system to guide her to the city—and the roads would be empty at this time. He'd easily be able to find another form of transport.

She bit her lip. True, he wouldn't be best pleased that she'd taken his car without asking—but it wouldn't be the first rule of etiquette she'd broken. Sleeping with the boss without him ever having taken her on a date was right up there with the major social no-nos.

It might be completely out of character, but so what? Things couldn't really get much worse. Her contract with Palladio's would inevitably be over after this—so what did she have to lose? And what the hell would Suzy, her partner, have to say about *that*?

Her cheeks burning with remorse, Aisling crept back into Gianluca's bedroom, breathing a sigh of relief as she located his car keys in the back pocket of his discarded jeans and carefully extracted them—and still he slept on.

She stole towards the front door and her heart pounded with guilt and she quietly took from her bag a pen and a postcard of the Trevi fountain, which she'd never got around to posting. Silently, she wrote: 'I've borrowed your car—will leave it at your office.'

And then she hesitated. How should she end it? *Love* Aisling?

No.

Just her name, then?

No. Just stick to facts and fade away into the dawn. Propping the note onto a small table, she gave a wry smile. Why, he might even thank her for it. They would both be spared the embarrassment of the morning after. The long, shared journey back to the city, heavy with awkward silences. Not that she'd ever had a one-night stand—but from everything she'd read, she knew it wasn't the best way to earn his respect or admiration.

But it wasn't until she was out on the open road, being guided by the rather spooky robotic female voice of the sat-nav system and heading towards Rome that she dared to put her foot down, her heart sinking with the horror of what she'd done as the sun began to rise high over the Umbrian hills.

CHAPTER FOUR

AISLING'S head pounded.

Unsteadily, she rose from her chair to close the blinds in her office, and the unanswerable question spun round and round in her head like dirty water whirling down the plug-hole.

Oh, what had she *done*?

Nearly a month had elapsed since she had woken up in Gianluca's bed—or rather *on* Gianluca's bed, she corrected herself, and flinched. There was no point in giving the incident an air of respectability which it certainly didn't merit. Saying that they had been *in* bed might have implied that there'd been a little forethought about that wild bout of sex, instead of the stark and unpalatable truth.

That she'd had a one-night stand with a client!

Aisling's palms felt clammy as she sat down at her desk once more.

What kind of a woman did that? Risking everything she'd worked so hard for. Especially a woman who had known real poverty when she was growing up—who had learnt the hard way that you couldn't rely on anyone except yourself to earn a living.

Her mother had always put men before everything—even her daughter. Janie Armstrong had sacrificed everything in her futile search for love. Jobs had gone by the wayside and she and Aisling had moved around the country—relocating at the drop of a hat if there was some promise of emotional happiness, which had never seemed to materialise.

Time after time, Aisling had seen her mother let down by a man—and time after time she had repeated the same needy and dependent behaviour which had seemed to drive the men further away. As her beauty had faded, so had the opportunities—and that had bred a new desperation.

Aisling had vowed to be different. That was the reason she had slaved away to establish her business, why she had put her social life on hold, working long hours to build up her small but thriving firm which now employed three people. A firm she had been so proud of—but which must now surely be threatened by a single act of madness?

How terrifying it was to discover this dark and unknown side to her character. Maybe she carried more of her mother's traits than she had previously imagined.

After leaving Gianluca's vineyard, Aisling had caught the London-bound flight from Rome airport with minutes to spare. She'd left Gianluca's car in the underground car park of the Palladio Corporation, deposited the car keys with his bemused secretary and walked out with a feeling of terrible remorse making her cheeks sting pink.

Next there had been Jason to face—and that had been Aisling's first real test of mental determination. How much was it permissible to pretend when facing your young assistant, to whom you were supposed to be setting a good example? She didn't want to lie—but how could she tell him the truth when, if the situation were reversed, she would have sacked him on the spot? There was nothing to be gained from showing her embarrassment and her guilt—she was just going to have to live with them. As it was, her former prim and proper image stood her in good stead.

'Whatever happened to you?' Jason asked curiously. 'One minute you were there—and the next you were gone!'

'Oh, Gianluca gave me a tour of the property—and we ended up talking about business,' she answered quietly, her blue eyes just daring him to say any more on the subject, and to her relief he didn't. Quite what Jason thought about it all only added to her discomfiture, but frankly she couldn't allow herself the luxury of wallowing in self-pity.

For days, Aisling waited.

At first she wasn't really sure what she was waiting for—until she woke up one morning after a night spent tossing and turning and realised that she was in fact waiting to hear from Gianluca. They still had a meeting scheduled to discuss his Miami project, didn't they? Her guilty conscience had made her assume that he would want to pull out of it—and that he would take great delight in telling her exactly why. But she was wrong.

There was nothing. Not a word, a phone call or e-mail to cancel—and somehow this only compounded her silent sense of agony and self-recrimination. Was he planning to send someone else from the Palladio Corporation in his place? she wondered.

And it wasn't until her period arrived that Aisling realised she had been waiting for something else, too—

the reassurance that there weren't to be any lasting repercussions from that night of passion. And thank God, there weren't.

But her behaviour made her think—logically, rather than emotionally. It shocked her into making an appointment at the family planning clinic. Because, yes, Gianluca had used protection—but what if he hadn't had any? She had been so caught up in mindless need for him that she'd been beyond caring—and, whether or not that was the Palladio effect, she didn't dare risk it happening again. A one-night stand was bad enough—an unplanned pregnancy would be unforgivable. And then there was the troublesome question of their upcoming appointment and how she might react if Gianluca turned up and tried to seduce her. Would she honestly be able to resist him?

The phone on her desk rang and Aisling picked it up.

'Aisling Armstrong here,' she said.

It was Ginger Jones, her secretary, who had taken to looking at her with frowning concern ever since she'd returned from Rome, even if she hadn't quite had the nerve to ask her if anything was wrong. Unlike Suzy, who had been fishing like mad—but Aisling had deflected all *her* questions without blushing.

'There's someone here to see you,' Ginger announced.

Aisling frowned as she scanned the appointments page of her diary. 'But I don't have anything scheduled.' And it was almost seven o'clock. It had been a long day, which had started with a breakfast meeting, and she wanted nothing more than a bath and to pick at some food and then go to bed and pray for the oblivion of sleep.

'I know that,' said Ginger rather dramatically, and something in the tone of her voice made the small hairs on the back of Aisling's neck prickle with apprehension.

'Who is it?' she questioned hoarsely.

'Signor Palladio.'

Aisling gripped the phone so hard that her knuckles turned the colour of milk. 'But his appointment isn't until next week,' she said hoarsely. An appointment she had been expecting and praying that he would cancel. *And praying that he wouldn't.*

'So I believe,' said Ginger smoothly.

'Can't you tell him to go?' Aisling whispered, and to Ginger's huge credit and diplomacy she didn't seem to find anything wrong in a question which Aisling would never have asked under normal circumstances.

'I've tried,' Ginger said, in a smoothly unfamiliar tone which suggested that the Italian billionaire might be standing right by the telephone.

Aisling thought quickly.

If she wanted to play French farce, she could always slip out of her office by the back way, but that would only postpone the inevitable. Gianluca obviously wanted to see her and he wouldn't be deterred—not by anyone. So hadn't she better listen to what he wanted to say?

Aisling chewed the end of her fountain pen. 'Won't you send him in?' she asked.

She put the receiver down and sat with the tension building up inside her. There wasn't even enough time to look in the mirror she carried in her handbag, nor to put on some lipstick—and, besides, it was only a short journey from Ginger's office to her own.

What if he caught her prettifying herself and thought she

was trying to lure him into another sexual encounter? Aisling shuddered as—like someone caught in a bad horror film—she watched the door open and her heart sank.

For this was the man they called *Il Tigre* at his most threatening, looking just as she imagined his animal namesake might look the moment before it pounced.

Gianluca closed the door behind him, but he didn't move. Just stood there, looking at her with a hostile black gaze—which was making her feel like some helpless innocent who had strayed into his path.

So don't *let* him make you feel that way.

But it wasn't easy under the circumstances—not when her heart was leaping against her ribcage in reaction to the muscular body and the shadowed beauty of his face—which was so still that it might have been carved from some dark stone. How could someone look so different? she wondered. It seemed a lifetime ago that those hard lips had been soft and responsive as they kissed her—yet it was only a few short weeks.

She tried to compose her face into some appropriate expression—but what was appropriate, in the circumstances?

'Hello, Gianluca,' she said as calmly as she could manage.

He didn't return the greeting, just leaned back against the door, his hands moving down to rest on his hips, a movement Aisling tried not to react to, which wasn't easy since, not only was it vaguely intimidating—it also meant that he thrust his hips forward in a way that was completely provocative as well as evocative. And, oh, the memories came flooding back in all their glorious, golden beauty.

She swallowed, remembering images that she had been trying to block—of his eyes, tight-closed with pleasure.

The way he had breathed something exultant at the moment of his climax and the warm feel of his naked body next to hers. 'This is a…surprise.'

'Really?' he clipped out. He was angry. Correction. He was *furious*—with a strength of feeling he was neither used to, nor liked—and he hadn't quite worked out what was causing it. Was it because she had taken control of the situation by her sudden and totally unexpected disappearance? Or because he had been shocked to find she had gone, leaving his bed without a single word—leaving him lying alone amid the rumpled sheets as if he were just some kind of *stud*!

Yet the sight of her was making him ache, even though in theory it should have done the very opposite—because the woman who had writhed beneath him and slid all over him had disappeared, making him half wonder whether he had imagined the whole episode. Like a shooting star viewed in the night sky—brilliant yet so dazzlingly brief.

Gone was the floaty hairstyle and the foxy jeans—and back in place was one of her mannish suits with her dark hair so tightly pinned back that she might as well have had it shaved off.

'Is this how you always behave?' he demanded. 'Don't you usually hang around to say goodbye to your lovers, Aisling—or do you consider orgasm as a kind of farewell as well as the little death which the French always use to describe it?'

'Shh! Please—keep your voice down!' The words were out before she could stop them and Aisling's gaze darted nervously towards the closed door, praying that Ginger didn't have her ear pressed to it. 'I don't want anyone to hear.'

'You don't want anyone to hear?' He gave a mocking laugh of derision, but also a mental note of her vulnerability, and what had provoked it. 'You mean you haven't told your secretary you've been sleeping with one of the clients?'

'Of course I haven't!' she retorted, until she realised that she was playing this all wrong. Calm it down, she told herself. Calm it *down.* Surely her disappearance should have set his mind at rest—made him realise that she wasn't going to make a big deal out of it?

She tried the kind of smile that she imagined a sophisticated woman-of-the-world might turn onto one of her many lovers. 'Anyway, there's nothing to tell, is there?' she finished brightly.

'Nothing to tell?' he echoed incredulously. 'You let me take your clothes off and to enter your body and move inside you and bring you to orgasm and yet you describe this as *nothing*?'

'Gianluca!' Her cheeks flared with heat, and with the first heavy beat of desire. *'Please!'*

'*Sì? Che cosa hai?* What is the matter with you?' His mouth twisted with fury and with something else too—something which felt bizarrely close to jealousy. 'Do you do this all the time, with different men? Different *clients*?' he finished insultingly.

The accusation was like a knife-wound and Aisling gripped at the desk. 'I don't—of course I don't! You can't think that!'

'Why not? Why should I believe you?'

Accusation blazed from his black eyes and Aisling felt weak. He really *did* think she was some kind of unprincipled pleasure-seeker! 'Believe me if you want, or don't!' she said. 'I don't have to pass some kind of a morality test—especially with a man like *you*!'

There was a moment's silence. 'And what exactly is *that* supposed to mean?' he questioned softly.

'Oh, come on, Gianluca—don't try to play the innocent with me. You're an intelligent man!' Her words were tumbling out thick and fast and Aisling could feel the threatening break of tears at the edge of them and wondered what had happened to her determination to stay calm.

Think of everything you've worked for, Aisling—don't throw it away in a crazy moment of turbulent emotion.

Yet she couldn't seem to stop herself, and maybe it was the cold, hurtful expression in his eyes—as if she had done something unspeakably wrong, instead of simply opting for damage limitation to avoid an awkward scene the following morning.

She swallowed away the threat of tears and drew a deep breath to steady herself. 'Maybe *you* make love to lots of different women like that?'

'Make *love*?' His laugh was scornful. '*Cara*, please! I implore you not to dress it up into something it wasn't. That had nothing to do with love, and everything to do with raw sex.'

Aisling recoiled, twisting her fingers together in her lap and digging the nails sharply into the fleshy part of her palm. She had known that all along and yet to hear him say so was oddly and profoundly wounding. And this was what she had feared, what she had warned herself she must never do—to read more into what had happened than he intended her to. Thank heaven she had left when she did—taken the upper hand instead of being shown the door and made to feel like some fallen woman.

'Why are you here?' she whispered.

Why indeed? Because he had woken up alone in bed the next morning, aching to possess her once more—only to discover the space where she had lain was empty? She had gone.

Gianluca was used to ending it where affairs were concerned…and then only when his appetite had been fully sated. And this time it had not. It had not just left him wanting her—it had left him wanting her *more*. For once, he felt at some kind of disadvantage and he didn't like it. He didn't like it at all. His mouth flattened into an implacable line—he wanted to lash out at her for the frustration he still felt.

'You took my *car*,' he said coldly.

Aisling's heart kicked against her ribcage, hating herself for the terrible wave of disappointment which washed over her. What had she been expecting him to say? That he'd wanted to carry on holding her? That she was the kind of woman he'd spent his life waiting for? Oh, you idiot, Aisling. 'How like a man,' she lashed back. 'To worry about his precious car.'

'It's not about the damned car!' he gritted. 'You made me look a *fool*! I woke in the morning and thought that you must have gone for a walk before breakfast.' He shook his head as he remembered. 'I went downstairs to find you but none of the maids had seen you. They looked at me in confusion, and then with embarrassment when they showed me your note.'

'So you were worried about your reputation?' Aisling queried acidly.

'A concept which clearly does not concern *you*.' He enjoyed seeing her wince—damn it, she could wince some more!

'I left the car at your office,' she defended. 'I only borrowed it.'

'You shouldn't have taken it in the first place!'

'Maybe I shouldn't—but what was I supposed to do? I had a flight to catch.'

He raised haughty black eyebrows in a gesture of disbelief. 'You don't think that I would have driven you back to Rome—or got you onto another flight? Or even chartered a plane to take you back to London?'

Aisling stared unseeingly at the neat, uncluttered expanse of her desk. How incongruous it would sound if she told him that she'd awoken with a feeling of shame that she could have so compromised their professional relationship. And she had panicked, wanting to keep what little was left of the tatters of her pride. Running away had seemed the only way out at the time.

Deep down she had known that she'd behaved badly—but now she could see that she had thrown a poor light on more than her reputation. Because a woman who so bitterly regretted having taken a lover would look like a very indiscriminate woman indeed…

'I'm sorry I ran out like that. I'm sorry I took the car,' she said baldly and looked up into the cold black eyes. 'There. You have your apology. What else do you want me to do about it?'

Conflicting thoughts began to spin around in his head and for once in his life, Gianluca wasn't sure.

He wanted to tell her to go to hell!

But he also wanted her to lift her hand and unclip her hair and let it fall all around her shoulders and…and…

He stifled a groan. Ultimately, what did he really want?

Yet he knew the answer to this. It had been eating away at him for weeks—ever since he had realised that she had no intention of contacting him again. A woman he had bedded not begging for more!

At first, he hadn't believed it—he had thought that she was playing a game of cat and mouse, as women tended to. But no. The expected, slightly awkward phone call had not come—nor the e-mail purporting to be about business, but with a tell-tale ending like: *It was great to see your vineyard…and if ever you're over in London…*

Nothing! And like all men who had always had their every whim and hunger indulged—to be denied something was uniquely appealing. Did she know that? Was she playing some kind of elaborate game with him—knowing all the right buttons to press? Thinking that if she gave him just a taster and then retreated, he would be prowling round her like an alley-cat?

She was the best head-hunter he had ever employed, but this had nothing to do with her skill at *that*. He wanted to possess her one last time—enough to let her go without a backward glance—but he recognised that he was going about it the wrong way. The woman who sat behind the desk was now on her own territory and it wasn't quite so easy to call the shots.

But she still worked for him, didn't she?

For the first time since he'd walked into her office, he moved away from the door towards her, seeing her pupils dilate at the same time as her fingers flew up to her throat in an instinctive gesture of sexual awareness, and his mouth twisted into a hard smile.

Did she think he was just going to go over to her and take her in his arms? With a certainty which had never failed him, he knew that if he began to kiss her then he would soon have her parting her legs and pleading with him to take her there and then.

The heavy beat of desire throbbed deep in his groin and briefly he contemplated taking such an action, but decided against it. Such a victory would be meaningless. The submission of her body too easy. She would submit with her mind and she would submit willingly! She wanted him, no matter what she protested to the contrary—and wouldn't the triumph of such a conquest quell his anger as well as his desire?

'Actually I wanted to talk to you about work,' he said softly.

The taut sexual tension in the air shattered like a bubble being pierced by a needle and Aisling's mouth opened and then closed again, his words taking her completely by surprise. 'Work?' she echoed dully.

Black eyes seared around her office like a laser-gun. *'Sì, cara,'* he drawled sarcastically. 'Work—that well-known four-letter word.' His black gaze lanced into her and taunted her. 'Shame on you, Aisling—has all your ambition deserted you? Sapped by a night of sex? I mean, I know I'm good—but *that* good? You *are* still in business, I suppose? I take it you still have staff wages to pay?'

'Well, yes—of course I do. It's just that I didn't…' Her voice trailed off, in a way which wasn't her usual style at all.

'Didn't what, Aisling?' he probed softly, wondering

what had made those ice-blue eyes suddenly grow darker—or could he guess?

She swallowed. 'I wasn't sure whether you'd still be wanting my services—' She flinched. Of all the explanations she could have chosen, that must have been the worst—and, judging from his slow smile, he was enjoying every second of her discomfiture.

So pull yourself together. Stop letting *him* control the show.

For the first time since he'd walked into her office, she fixed him with a defiant look. 'I wasn't sure whether we would continue to be working together, in view of what happened.'

But even as she said the words Aisling realised how much the world must have turned upside down for her to even consider losing him.

If she lost Gianluca's account, then she couldn't afford to employ young Jason—and how would it make her feel to think that a promising young graduate could be thrown on the scrap heap simply because she'd allowed sexual hunger to sway her judgement?

Aisling's business meant pretty much everything to her, and rightly so. It was her baby—and, the way things were panning out in her life, it was probably the only baby she was ever going to have. If she carried on the way she was doing, it would eventually provide her with the security she'd always yearned for. That was her target, anyway.

Was she really prepared to throw her most prestigious contract away, simply because she had allowed an ill-considered passion to take root? Especially if he seemed prepared to forget what had happened.

He was watching her closely—could see the indecision criss-crossing her pale face. 'Oh, come on, Aisling. You said yourself, it's nothing. And if it's nothing, then it shouldn't affect our professional relationship, should it?'

Aisling bit her lip. Could she go through with it—working with him again under this startling new set of circumstances? 'You want to discuss the Miami project?' she questioned.

'No, *cara*. I do not. There is a hold-up with the planning application and so for the moment it's not moving.'

So why was he here? 'You mean there's another job in the offing?' she asked, her professional interest aroused in spite of the bizarre circumstances.

Gianluca gave a slow smile. So the lure had worked, just as he had known it would. The ice-queen would be unable to resist business, wouldn't she? 'Of course—and it's an even bigger project. I've been in London all week on business. Why else did you think I was here?' He glittered her a questioning look. 'Surely you didn't think I'd flown over especially to see you?'

'No, of course not.' Now she felt stupid. And hurt, too. *Had* she thought that? And he'd been in the same city for a whole week without contacting her... She tried to keep her voice steady, but it wasn't easy. 'What kind of project?' she asked.

He had thought about taking her out to dinner and then to bed, but now thought better of it. Let her wait and let her wonder. Let her drive herself crazy all night long remembering how it had felt to have Gianluca Palladio make love to her—and let her body ache for him until he was ready to make his move once more!

Deliberately, he glanced at his watch. 'It's getting late, and I'm tired. We'll talk about it tomorrow.'

Their eyes met in a clash of wills.

'And if I refuse?'

His smile was as cold as marble. 'Then I will take your professional reputation and I will destroy it,' he said, in a soft voice. 'Be very sure of that, *cara*.'

CHAPTER FIVE

'SHALL I show Signor Palladio in now?' questioned Ginger.

'Just give me five minutes, will you, Ginger?' Aisling gave a grim kind of smile as she flicked up the switch of the intercom. This time he could wait. This time she wouldn't buckle beneath his domineering ways. If they really were to continue working together, then he was going to have to show her a little respect—no matter what had gone on that night in Italy. *Il Tigre* wouldn't scare *her*.

She would finish her coffee and reapply her lipstick and generally psych herself up to greet him. As if that might somehow magically repair the damage of a largely sleepless night.

Aisling gazed into the mirror. There were dark shadows smudged beneath her eyes and her face was pale. But so what—she wasn't trying to impress him, was she? *Was* she?

Smoothing her fingers down over the already smooth cap of her hair, she went back to her desk, took a deep breath and buzzed Ginger.

'Would you send Signor Palladio in now?'

'Sure thing!'

Was it Aisling's imagination, or did her assistant sound

a little *giddy*? But then the door opened and Ginger came in with an expression of such pleasure on her face that anyone would have thought she'd just won the national lottery. No, it hadn't been Aisling's imagination at all.

'I'll go and get you both some coffee,' Ginger said, beaming up at Gianluca.

'I don't remember asking for any,' said Aisling mildly.

Ginger wriggled her pale-green cashmere-clad shoulders and the titian hair which had provided her nickname shimmied all the way down her back. 'No, but Gianluca looked so…*tired*…that I offered to make him some.'

Ginger was *gushing*, thought Aisling furiously. She was actually *gushing*! And just when had she been given permission to start calling him by his Christian name? 'Thank you,' she said crisply, and as the door closed behind her secretary Aisling dared look him in the eyes for the first time.

In a way it was easy to see why Ginger had been so uncharacteristically simpering towards him. He was dressed in a pale grey suit, which accentuated the golden glow of his skin and the jet-black gleam of his hair. The shadow around his jaw was fainter than usual and his black eyes were brilliant and gleaming.

He seemed so *alive*—exuding an air of vitality which set him apart from the usual men she met. Was it any wonder that she had acted the way she had?

'Your assistant is very cute, *cara*,' murmured Gianluca, who had watched the little exchange between the two women with amusement.

'She's very good at her job,' said Aisling defensively, and to her horror she felt a violent stab of something like envy.

He assumed an expression of shock. 'Did I say she

wasn't?' he protested. 'Just because a woman is warm and giving towards a man, doesn't mean that she's in any way inadequate.'

Was that a dig at her? And was she going to react to it? No, she was not. Aisling picked up her fountain pen and twirled it around between her perfectly manicured fingers like a mini-baton.

'Won't you sit down?' she said coolly, watching as he spread his elegant frame in the chair and made it look as substantial as a piece of dolls' house furniture. 'And then we can discuss what you have in mind.'

He allowed himself the idle fantasy of telling her that what he really had in mind was to rip that horrible skirt from her body and to press his tongue into the little dip in the centre of her belly and to lick her there until she gasped with pleasure.

She stared at him with polite question in her eyes and reluctantly he dragged his thoughts away from the silken softness of her thighs to the infinitely more mundane subject of his recent takeover.

'You remember that I said I was thinking of expanding further in England?'

Aisling nodded.

'Well, the opportunity to do just that presented itself to me recently.' He paused. 'I'm in the process of buying a hotel and it's all been very hush-hush. I would prefer you to say nothing until the official announcement is made.'

'Oh?' Concentrate on what he's saying to you, and not on the high, proud slash of his cheekbones. 'Which hotel?'

'It's the Vinoly,' he said, seeing her blue eyes widen.

Aisling blinked. 'You mean the Vinoly in central London?'

'I wasn't aware there was more than one.'

'Good heavens!' she said faintly, putting the pen down on the desk. 'It's one of the city's most famous landmarks!' She blinked again. 'In fact—it's practically an *institution*.'

'But of course. That's why I wanted it.'

Aisling gave a dry laugh. 'Just like that?'

'Why not? Acquisitions excite me.'

Something about the way he said it unsettled her. All successful businessmen were constantly seeking out the new. Like sharks, they were never still—the very best of them always looking out to make a killing, because you never stayed at the top by remaining stagnant.

Maybe that attitude had spilled over into his private life, too. Was that why he had never settled down with one woman—because he conducted his private life on a similar scale? Had she just been another, rather unexpected 'acquisition'?

Angrily, she straightened the pen, so that it lay at a perfect right angle to the blotter. *This* was why people didn't have affairs at work—because you started to think about everything in how it related to *you*, instead of how it related to the business!

'Is something wrong, Aisling?' he murmured.

'Wrong? No. Why should anything be wrong?'

He shrugged, but, oh, he was enjoying this—watching Little Miss Prim try not to react to him and failing hopelessly. 'You were *glaring*.'

'Was I?' She shrugged right back and met his eyes defiantly. 'Probably because I often glare when I concentrate.'

'I see.'

Was he *laughing* at her? wondered Aisling furiously.

There was a knock on the door and Ginger brought in a tray of coffee. Aisling noted that, not only had she made a whole potful of the stuff, but she must have nipped out to the deli next door for some of their fancy biscuits.

'What a lot of trouble you have gone to, Ginger,' murmured Gianluca.

Had he deliberately exaggerated his accent to make the first syllable of her name rhyme with 'jean'? wondered Aisling. And did Ginger really have to bat her eyelashes at him like some amateur vamp as she breathed out her breathless response?

'Oh, it's no trouble, Gianluca!'

Aisling wondered how he would have reacted if he had been given a mugful of the rather mediocre instant coffee which was what they *usually* drank, but she didn't say anything. She waited until the door had closed behind her before picking up the pot and forcing her mind back to his hotel. 'The Vinoly,' she mused. 'Second biggest hotel in London after the Granchester, and an architectural gem. I guess congratulations must be in order.'

His dark eyes narrowed thoughtfully. 'You sound doubtful,' he observed.

'Well, it's a bit of a departure for you. You usually deal in smaller, boutique hotels.' She poured him a cup of coffee and pushed it across the desk in front of him. 'Biscuit?'

He shook his head.

Aisling poured her own. 'Won't this affect the industry's view of you? Isn't it a slightly risky strategy?'

Gianluca stared at her with something approaching admiration—at her icy blue eyes which gave away precisely nothing. Had he been expecting her to be cowed by his insistence on this meeting? Perhaps for her to display irritation towards the secretary who was so obviously flirting with him? Or maybe to gush just a little, recognising that a man who could afford to buy the Vinoly must be a very rich man indeed—and he knew only too well how most women responded to wealth.

And hadn't there been a tiny part of his mind which had wondered whether she might behave as other women in her position might have done? That, having known the pleasures of his body, she might lock the office door and slide off her panties and come over here and sit on his lap…

But no—the expression she presented to him was completely professional and the objections she voiced were exactly as they should be. And the cool expression on her face was starting to make him wonder whether he'd actually dreamt the whole seduction.

As a client he applauded it, while as a man, it irritated the hell out of him. There had been not one intimation—not a single hint—that they had shared a night of passion in his bed, and in truth he found that deeply insulting. Did she have no *feelings*?

His mouth hardened. Perhaps she imagined that by remaining so composed in his presence she would make him want her even more.

And she was right, damn her!

He was the one who usually compartmentalised—and it was not a trait he particularly admired in the opposite sex. He liked his women warm and soft and available—ready to juggle their schedules to fit in with *his* busy life.

He sipped the coffee, which was surprisingly good, finding himself in the curious position of having to force his mind back to work instead of the memory of her pale, curving body revealed by his removal of that rather plain underwear.

'You are doubting my ability to expand into this particular market?' he demanded.

'No, of course I'm not. And I can find whoever you need to staff it. I assume you'll want a new general manager—someone who will put your own particular stamp on the place?'

'*Sì*. But I don't want to change too much, too quickly.' His eyes narrowed thoughtfully. 'I want to be able to observe what works and what doesn't, before I decide.'

Aisling hesitated. 'You'll be careful not to change *too* much, won't you, Gianluca? One of the place's biggest selling points is its very Britishness—the tourists love all that.'

She was unbelievable! 'You think that I'll serve only pizza in the restaurants from now on and start playing loud Italian opera?' he queried sarcastically.

'And plastic gondolas on sale in the foyer,' she agreed, deadpan.

His mouth twitched as he tried to hold back a smile. 'Ah, Aisling,' he sighed. 'What is it that you object to in this deal?'

He paid for her judgement and her perception, didn't he? And for the truth, too.

'It's just that this a departure from the Palladio brand,' she said softly. 'That's all.'

'A *brand*?' he echoed. 'You think that Gianluca Palladio is a *brand*? What kind of a word is that? You are comparing me to a can of beans, perhaps?'

'Oh, don't be so melodramatic, Gianluca—of course I'm not! I'm just telling you not to lose that special something for which you're known.'

'Ah!' His eyes narrowed and a sudden sensation of friction became almost tangible in the air around them. His voice dipped. 'And what special something would that be?'

Feeling as if she'd walked straight into a trap of her own making, Aisling felt her skin grow warm—the tightening of her breasts reminding her all too clearly of Gianluca the lover. How he had suckled them, teased them with his teeth, licked them.

She bit her lip. Oh, *why* remember something at a time like this? The colour in her cheeks intensified and she found she wanted to look away from him, but couldn't. She swallowed. 'Gianluca. Please, don't.'

'Don't what, *cara*? Don't desire you when it feels as natural to me as breathing? Don't you know how lovely you look when you lose that frosty look of yours and smile? I saw you smile more times in my arms that night than I've done in almost two years of working with you.'

'But that's not why we're here!' she said quickly. 'What happened that night was a moment of madness—a mistake.'

He stared at her disbelievingly. 'And that's all?'

'That's all,' she agreed. Because what alternative did she have? Admit she'd done nothing but think about him—with images of his mocking face and hard body consuming her memory like a fever? 'And we're supposed to be working,' she reminded him. 'I'm your head-hunter and you asked my opinion.'

There was a pause but all he could think was how tantalising it was to be pushed away. 'I know you are,' he said softly. 'And that's why I want you to come to a cocktail party at the Vinoly this evening. This will be a good opportunity to observe how the hotel is being run with a degree of relative anonymity. Once the sale goes through it will be impossible for me to fade in the background.'

Aisling swallowed. She felt he was playing with her. Pushing her around like a croupier sliding little plastic chips across a gaming table. 'But if you take me with you, then won't people guess?'

'And what will they guess, *cara*?' he taunted. 'That we're lovers, or that I'm buying the hotel?'

'But we're not lovers, Gianluca. Not any more.'

He smiled, but the curve of his lips was cynical and it made a perfect partner for the mockery in his eyes. *Aren't we?* they seemed to say. 'It's at six, in the Thames Room. I'll send a car here for you.'

She shook her head in frustration, feeling control begin to slip away, and it scared her. 'I'm a London girl and I'm used to getting around the city on my own. There's really no need to—'

He cut across her protest with an arrogant wave of his hand.

'I will send a car,' he repeated obstinately.

CHAPTER SIX

AISLING remembered the first time she'd ever been to the Vinoly, with its sweeping mahogany staircase and famous rooftop restaurant. She'd been an impressionable twenty year old who hadn't yet learnt that it was almost impossible to hold a drink as well as eat a canapé, and she had ended up squashing a filo-pastry case against her best dress and ruining it.

These days, of course, she never ate canapés—and had lots of dresses which could have been defined as 'best', all hanging in neatly pressed, plastic-shrouded lines in the wardrobe of her apartment. She was also used to London's more glamorous locations and conducted many of her meetings at this particular venue.

Nonetheless, when the luxurious black car dropped her off at the revolving doors of the famous hotel, she felt the nerves which were beginning to gnaw away at her. Not that anyone would have guessed it from the cool, calm smile on her face. In fact, no one would have guessed anything.

She knew a million ways to hide what she was feeling—she had learnt them at about the same time she'd learnt to ride a bike. You developed a pretty tough skin when you were instructed to tell the creditors that your mother had nipped out to the shops and you didn't know when she'd be back.

Her high heels sinking into the acres of plush carpet, she walked along the seemingly endless corridors towards the venue. She could hear the chatter of voices as she walked into the crowded Thames Room, and then she saw Gianluca and her heart seemed to stand still.

He was surrounded by people who were trying not to look as if they were jostling for his attention, but that was exactly what they were doing—especially some of the women were circling him like a pack of glossy predators. And you are *not* going to join their desperate ranks, she told herself calmly.

Gianluca glanced up and saw her and something about her quiet poise captured his attention. She was wearing a simple pink silk dress—with a pair of plain pearl studs her only adornment. She gave him a small, polite nod of recognition and he felt his fingers tighten around his glass of champagne as she began to walk towards him.

Over the last few weeks he had found himself thinking about that night in Umbria. Wondering if her behaviour that night had been a bizarre one-off—something completely out-of-character, which would never be repeated. Or if maybe she was a game-player—knowing that a man of his experience liked nothing more than a challenge. Had she read one of those books which advised women that the best way to hook a powerful man was to keep him guessing?

'Aisling,' he murmured as she approached. 'You made it.'

She met his eyes. 'Did I have a choice?'

He gave a quick, hard smile. 'No.'

Aisling forced herself to look around because anything was safer than gazing into his eyes. 'It's certainly crowded.'

'You like cocktail parties?'

She shrugged. 'Not really. They're an occupational hazard, aren't they?'

'Like plane journeys, you mean?'

'Well, yes. Or meetings with the bank manager.'

'Ah, but I have someone else do those for me.'

'Well, aren't you the lucky one!'

Now their eyes met. '*Sì*,' he murmured. 'Aren't I just?'

'Gianluca!'

A woman's voice shattered the air like a stone being hurled through a window, but Aisling was grateful for the interruption. Her heart was hammering and she felt positively weak. How could a few meaningless words seem so…so *significant*?

Because you want them to be significant. Because he's experienced and you're not, that's why. And if you allow him to flirt with you, then you're playing with fire.

'Gianluca!' said the voice again and Aisling found herself elbowed out of the way by a blonde with astonishingly green eyes and gravity-defying breasts.

She needed to get away from him—because she didn't *want* to stand there, companionably sharing similar views on cocktail parties and air-travel. Soon she would start thinking that they were compatible—and they *weren't*. She took a step back. 'Look, I mustn't monopolise you any more, Gianluca. You will excuse me, won't you?'

With something approaching shock, Gianluca realised that she was actually walking away. In fact, she was smiling at a couple of people *en route* and had begun making her way towards the wall of glass at the other side of the room, which overlooked the view of the river

Thames. Leaving him with the kind of woman he could see was going to display all the staying power of a leech.

'I went to Italy once and absolutely fell in love with it!'

His eyes narrowed as he realised that the blonde was talking to him, but he'd barely heard a word she'd been saying. He stared at her, as if she had suddenly appeared out of nowhere. Didn't she realise that if a woman thrust her breasts into your face it was like being offered a meal when you had just eaten?

Abruptly, he excused himself, but then bumped into a visiting Italian opera star he hadn't seen for years and was then introduced to a Minister of State. Every time he tried to break free, another VIP was foisted upon him, and all the time he was watching Aisling out of the corner of his eye, noticing the way she was networking.

What was it about her that made him unable to tear his eyes away from her tonight? Was it simply because she was frustrating the hell out of him?

The party was beginning to fold by the time he walked towards her pink-clad back, wondering if he should shake off this sense of persistence and put the whole thing down to experience. If he left now—would he really care? If he never had sex with her again, surely it wouldn't matter. Wouldn't the next woman wash her from his memory?

Yet his eyes were drawn to her neck, its long, slim column exposed by the severe chignon, and he found himself wanting to whisper his lips all the way down it. To bite the soft lobe of one of those perfect ears and whisper into it that he wanted her.

'You seem to make a habit of turning your back on me,' he observed acidly. 'Why didn't you stay?'

Aisling kept her expression bland as she faced him. 'By your side?' Her eyes travelled over his shoulder to where the blonde was staring rather disconsolately in his direction. 'You looked like you were fully occupied.'

'That isn't the point,' he said softly. 'You're supposed to be here tonight, working for me.'

'And that's exactly what I *have* been doing! If you really want me to give you my opinion of how I think the hotel is being run these days, then I can certainly accomplish it better by working the room on my own. Rather than being constantly watched by the spectators,' she added, glancing across the room to where the blonde had been joined by a popular soap actress, 'who seem to be following your every move.'

Gianluca smiled. 'Jealous?'

'Don't flatter yourself.'

'The irony is that I don't usually need to,' he said coolly. 'But I take your point, *cara*—and you must have seen enough by now. So let's go and have dinner. I've booked the Starlight.'

He saw her lips part but he shook his head. 'No,' he said flatly. 'Because the more you fight me, the more determined I become to get my own way.' He let his gaze drift over her flushed face. 'If it was anyone else but me, then you'd agree to dinner straight away—because that's the sort of business you operate in. You can't make exceptions just *because* it's me, *cara*. And you really shouldn't sleep with your clients if you feel that it is going to compromise your ability to do your job properly.'

'That's a bastard thing to say,' she whispered.

He felt a heady thrill at her reaction. 'And I don't think calling your boss names in public is setting a very good example, do you?'

'Whereas issuing veiled threats is textbook behaviour, I suppose?' she retaliated.

Better and better! 'If it's the only way of getting what I want, *cara*, then I'll do it. So be nice.' He reached out and touched his finger to the tip of her nose, seeing her blue eyes grow startled.

But just what *did* he want? Aisling wondered dazedly as they left the ballroom and headed towards the lift. She felt he was playing games with her—as a cruel kind of sport, perhaps? And the trouble was that she didn't know how to respond to them because the boundaries between them of work and play had become so blurred.

The Starlight restaurant was aptly named—an award-winning circular room of windows at the very top of the hotel. Outside, the crescent moon looked close enough to pluck from the night sky and below them lay the golden-bathed Houses of Parliament and the glittering snake of the river as it wound its way through the capital.

It was one of the most breathtaking views in London and Aisling stood for a moment, just staring down at it.

'Ever been here before?' he asked.

'Once. A long time ago.'

But back then she had been excited and impressed by the magical setting of the twinkling stars and the chance of spotting someone famous. Tonight was different. With Gianluca sitting opposite her, it was difficult to concentrate on anything and the richly romantic setting seemed to mock the curious nature of her brief affair with him. How did other women cope in such situations? she wondered. Did they instinctively know what to do—or, deep down, were they all flailing wildly and making up the rules as they went along?

Gianluca watched her studying the menu-card as if it were an examination paper, flickering his eyes over her bent head with a slight ache of amusement—realising that this was the first time in a long, long time that he had been forced to endure a dinner for the sake of propriety. 'What would you like?'

'Oh, I don't know—whatever it's best known for. Isn't there some kind of signature dish?'

He spoke to the waiter in French, ordered them both some fish and wine and waited while their drinks were poured. Then he leaned back in his chair and studied her. 'You do realise that you're still a complete mystery to me? That I've known you for almost two years, we've had sex together and yet I don't even know where you live?'

'Gianluca!'

'Doesn't that strike you as strange?' he questioned, ignoring her protest.

'There's never been a reason for you to know,' she said. 'There isn't really one now.'

He watched as she picked up her glass of water with a hand which wasn't quite steady. 'Being evasive won't work,' he said evenly. 'I'm curious.'

'Do you always interrogate when you're out on a date, Gianluca?'

'Is this a date, then, *cara*?'

Oh, but he managed to twist everything she said!

In the circumstances, it seemed bizarre to give him a potted life history—it seemed the wrong way round, really. They'd done the bed bit, without any of the getting-to-know-you stuff. But how else were they going to endure a whole meal together, if he was determined to find out and she was equally determined not to tell him? It would simply become a battle of wills, which she suspected he would win. 'I live in Putney.'

'By the river?' he observed. 'You must be doing well.'

'I'm actually about ten minutes' walk from the river and it's only a one-bedroomed apartment—but I love it. I've been trading up ever since I got a foothold on the property market.'

'And when was that?'

'As soon as I could afford to. I saved up like mad for a deposit. I hadn't really…'

Her words tailed off and he pounced on the rare chink in her armour. 'Hadn't really what?'

Surely if she made herself *sound* vulnerable, then she would make herself *seem* vulnerable? And what would *he* understand about savings, and deposits? Gianluca wasn't just rich, he had been born rich—everyone knew that. How could a man like that possibly relate to her story? 'I'd never lived anywhere that wasn't rented before,' she said reluctantly.

He raised his dark brows. 'Not even as a child?'

How few people had experienced it in the world she now occupied, she thought wryly. These days, in the UK, home ownership was seen as a right rather than a privilege, and Aisling gave a brittle smile. 'No, not even then,' she agreed, glad that the waiter chose that moment to bring a basket of bread, and hoping that Gianluca might let it go.

But he didn't.

'That's unusual for this country,' he said slowly.

'Not that unusual,' she contradicted. 'It's just that a lot of people never get out of the poverty trap and I was lucky that I did.'

'What happened?'

She hesitated. 'My mother was a single parent, without a proper career of her own.'

'And your father?'

'I never knew my father. He left before I was born.'

He frowned. 'So no stable male influence when you were growing up?'

'No.'

He filed the fact away. Was that why she didn't flirt and dress up like most women—because she didn't trust men, or she just didn't know how they operated? 'You never felt the need to trace him?'

'Never. I couldn't see the point. There.' She looked at him defiantly. 'End of subject.'

'That must have been hard for you,' he observed slowly.

But she wasn't asking for his sympathy. 'Put it this way—a few knocks on the way didn't do me any harm. It's what fed my ambition and my determination to be self-sufficient. And it's made me what I am. An independent woman.'

He affected a look of horror yet inside he felt an admiration for how she had coped, more than coped—succeeded—in a tough world by making a go of her own business. 'Don't you know how terrifying a man finds it when a woman describes herself as independent, *cara*?' he murmured.

'I can see it might bother a certain *type* of man.'

'What type?'

'Mr Macho,' she said flippantly.

He laughed. 'You can be outrageous,' he murmured.

And so could he. Her blue eyes challenged him. 'Look, Gianluca, fascinating as it is to discuss my life story, I thought you'd brought me up here to talk about business.'

Was she being deliberately naïve about his intentions, he wondered—or just playing a game? 'And maybe I've changed my mind. In truth, I'm a little distracted by the mass of contradictions you seem to be, Aisling. Maybe I want to get to know you a little better.'

She attempted an air of perplexity, but inside her heart was pounding. 'I can't see why.'

'Can't you? You have no curiosity beyond the physical act, is that it?' His voice roughened as he watched her face, enjoying the way her eyes darkened. 'We had a night of the most unexpectedly mind-blowing sex and yet you don't seem interested in a repeat performance.' His black eyes narrowed. 'And I can't for the life of me work out why.'

Maybe it was his use of the word 'performance' which rankled, or maybe it was just his arrogant assumption that any woman, having tasted the pleasures of his body, wouldn't be able to keep from coming for more—no matter the wear and tear it might inflict on a susceptible heart. 'Oh, can't you? Is that because your damned ego is so big?'

He was laughing now. 'Not my ego, *cara*, no.'

She felt the flame which flared over her cheeks and dropped her voice to a furious whisper. 'Do you want me to get up and walk out of this room right now?'

'Yes,' he retorted, his gaze imprisoning hers. 'If it means you'll come up to my suite and let me make love to you and damned well rid my blood of the fire you've lit within it.'

She stared at him in shock and the beating of her heart accelerated. 'Gianluca! What kind of a proposition is that?'

'One night,' he said flatly. 'Just one night. We finish off what was started in Italy. And that's it.'

'I can't believe what I'm hearing,' she breathed.

'No? Then I implore you to be honest with yourself, *cara*. The thought of you is driving me wild—and don't tell me you don't feel the same way, because I won't believe you. I can see it in your eyes, too—though you replace it with that icy coolness when you sense that I'm looking at you. But it's there, and you can't hide it. The hunger. The need—gnawing away inside you.'

'You make it sound like an…appetite.'

'Because that's exactly what it is.' He leaned forward, his expression intent, realising that this was at least one good thing about making a proposition to Aisling. At least she saw things in black and white and not dressed up in idealistic shades of make-believe. To a woman with such a good head for business—she would consider this a viable proposition.

'A hunger which can be fed and then forgotten,' he continued. 'We're colleagues. Neither of us want all the complications of a long-distance relationship—so why not draw a line under the whole affair in the most delightful way possible? We put it to bed, so to speak—and then forget it ever happened.'

Aisling stared into his beautiful face while her heart warred with her head, because it was never going to be up there with one of the Great Romantic Declarations, was it? And yet it was honest.

Some women might have found it insulting—so why didn't she? Was it because he hadn't made it out to be something it wasn't? He'd spoken nothing but the stark, unvarnished truth—and didn't that count for much more than the kind of empty promises which had seen her mother disappointed over and over again?

There had been no coyness between the two of them that night in Umbria—and that had been the most amazing night of her life. He was treating her as the independent woman she claimed to be. Speaking to her as an equal. Two grown-ups who both wanted each other. He had spoken of ridding himself of a fire in his blood—might she not do the same with this one night?

But what if she *couldn't* forget him?

In the flicker of the candlelight his eyes gleamed like jet and her heart turned over with longing. What if one night with this man wasn't enough? Didn't women operate differently from men and wasn't she running the risk of putting herself in the type of terrible emotional danger which she had always sought to avoid?

Yet what was the alternative? An unresolved desire which ran the risk of dominating her world and her life?

The waiter put two plates in front of them, but she barely noticed them.

'And if I agree—what about...afterwards?'

He gave an odd sort of smile. 'It will be gone. *Finito.* Remembered occasionally, no doubt—taken out and remembered as one might remember an especially delicious meal or a particularly beautiful holiday destination, but nothing more than that.'

She thought of the job she worked so hard for. Of the people who relied on her—of the security all those things gave her, that and the sense of being needed. She owed it to those people to put their needs before her own desires. 'And the contract?' she questioned.

There was a moment's silence and his mouth twisted. He had been right—she had nothing in the way of a heart!

'Oh, do not worry, Aisling, I have no intention of terminating your contract—of jeopardising your precious business—if that's all you're concerned about.'

His judgement was harsh and unfair and Aisling was hurt that he should have chosen to interpret her words like that. But perhaps it was better that he should think of her that way. As a kind of tough career-woman rather than the weak and vulnerable kind.

She shook her head. 'I don't know.'

How ironic it was to hear her sounding uncertain—she, whom he always thought of as so crisply decisive. Yet how deeply satisfying to see her wavering—to see those ice-blue eyes looking so unsure.

Gianluca leaned over towards her and traced the outline of her lips with his finger, and Aisling found her mouth opening so that he slid his finger inside it and she started with pleasure, and shock.

'See?' he mocked, and then he mouthed, *Suck me*.

And she did.

Their eyes met in a silent and erotic question.

'Come, Aisling,' he said softly as he withdrew his finger and looked at it, now all wet from her mouth. 'Before I die from wanting you. One night. No more.'

Her heart was beating so fast she felt dizzy. 'Our dinner—'

'Forget the damned dinner!'

She hesitated for one last second and then rose to her feet, taking the hand he offered before they both walked out of the restaurant—oblivious to the stares of the other diners or the waiter's expression of consternation on seeing the two untouched meals left behind on the table.

CHAPTER SEVEN

'TAKE down your hair,' Gianluca instructed silkily.

'No. *You* take it down.'

'Very well, *bella donna*!' And he began to untie Aisling's hair.

The walk to his suite had been the longest of his life and once inside Gianluca had imagined that he might just rip the clothes from her body—but no. Something had made him want to prolong the exquisite anticipation. Instead, he lifted his hand to remove pin after pin, so that streams of her hair fell like dark ribbons over her shoulders and breasts.

Gianluca let out a long sigh of pure desire as he watched it spill down like shadowy water. He had only seen it like this once before and then, as now, it seemed not only to symbolise her sexuality, but also to make her look softer and so much more feminine. Was that why she never normally wore it this way? 'Why do you hide it away?' he murmured.

'Because…' she swallowed, closing her eyes as he began to stroke his hand down over her hips, as if he were petting a cat '…it isn't practical when it's loose.'

'And are you always practical, *cara*?'

'Mostly.'

'This is a pity. Why?'

'It's called basic survival. But does it…' she gasped as he raked his fingers through the ebony tumble, his breath warm on her cheek as he brought her right up close to his hard body '…*matter*?'

No. Maybe not now. In fact, nothing seemed to matter right now other than his urgent need to kiss her.

But the long, leisurely kiss surprised him. Had he thought that he might just take her swiftly in order to appease the terrible sexual hunger which had been eating away at him for weeks? Yet here he was savouring every slow, delicious mouthful.

Aisling swayed—her eyes closing as she gave herself up to the sweetness of his lips. This time they weren't beneath a starry ceiling of Italian stars, serenaded by the massed choirs of cicadas—but this was still Gianluca of whom she had dreamed. In his arms she could surrender to the powerful ache of her own need and forget everything except pure pleasure.

And this time there were no hordes of people who might come spilling out of a party and catch them. This time they were alone.

The kiss changed—became deeper and more intense. He kissed her until there was no breath in his lungs, until he had to drag his mouth away from hers and suck in some much-needed air while he steadied himself. And then he groaned, running his hands luxuriantly over her silk-clad body.

'What is it that you do to me? For you are hot and cold—like the tap,' he breathed unsteadily. 'One minute the iceberg and the next—so sexy and so vibrant that it takes my breath away. Is this a clever game you play, Aisling?

For you are a clever woman. Do you do this to make me want you more?'

Surely it would be a mistake to tell him that it was uniquely *him* who could transform her into this wildly passionate creature? Wouldn't doing that only expose her vulnerability and appeal to his remarkable arrogance? And anyway—how could she think straight when his hands were stroking her like that? 'It's not a...game,' she stumbled.

'No?' He kissed her again, flicking his tongue into her mouth. Then what was it? When had he last felt like this? As if this were what he had been created for? Yet with this vitality came an odd and debilitating weakness—a feeling that she had him in her power—and Gianluca sought to wrest it back again, for no woman ever had supremacy over him.

He slid his hand further down, feeling her squirm beneath his fingers as he let it drift down to her thighs and then let out a small groan of dismay. 'You're wearing *tights*!' he accused hotly. 'Why not stockings?'

'Because they're impractical,' she breathed. 'And they can sometimes show, if you're not careful. Tights are much more suitable for a dress like this.'

'Not with legs like yours,' he murmured. But it interested him to think that she was wearing the biggest turn-off known to man. Which suggested that she had not come out tonight with seduction in mind. Either that, or she was playing a remarkably disingenuous game.

He brushed the silken ebony hair back from her pale skin and stared into the blue eyes. 'Shall I play a game with *you*?' he questioned unsteadily. 'Shall I take you now? Here? On the floor? Or up against the wall? Do you have any objections to that, *cara*?'

Aisling shook her head. Was he trying to shock her? To remind her that this meant nothing more than one night? Her knees weakened as she clung to his broad shoulders. Everything about him was designed to make her want him. The lean, hard body and the muscular shaft of his thigh which was pushing against hers. Only the clinical words jarred—but not enough to make her push him away.

'Shall I?' he murmured, skating a provocative little circle at the top of her thigh. 'Or shall I make you wait?'

But the way he was stroking her was making her tremble. 'No. Don't. Anything but that.' She shook her head as she moved her body distractedly against his. 'Please don't make me wait.' Because it seemed like an eternity since he had last held her like this.

His mouth was at her throat and he smiled with triumph at her eager capitulation. He could feel the pulse of her beating against his lips, her silk-covered breasts pressing against him, and he felt himself growing hard.

And suddenly he didn't want to wait, either. Couldn't wait. Not when she was writhing into him like that. Sensual little witch. Even *with* the tights. With an unexpectedly violent tug, he began to jerk down the side zip of the dress, but he felt a resistance and when he lifted his head to see that it was stuck, he swore in heated Italian. 'Do something,' he clipped out. 'Let me rip the whole damned thing off!'

She stared down at it, hot breath spilling out—tempted to tell him to go right ahead. But years of living from hand-to-mouth could not be overcome in a moment of passion and Aisling stayed his hand with her own. 'No!' she protested. 'These are the only clothes I have with me. And how can I possibly walk out of here in a ripped dress?'

'I will send out for a new one,' he stated arrogantly.

But his words only increased her resolve. She wasn't some little wannabe—eager to be fobbed off with Gianluca's charity in the form of a replacement wardrobe. She could buy her own clothes, thank you very much. She shook her head and began to fiddle around with the zip. 'No. Let me.'

Gianluca's eyes narrowed for a moment in anger and then he began to laugh. 'Ever the practical!' he mocked, but he watched as she freed the zip, and then carefully stepped out of the dress.

'I'd better go and hang this up,' she said.

He stared at her incredulously. Was she aware that no woman had ever broken the sexual mood quite so unashamedly with such a mundane little request? And yet the sheer *ordinariness* of the situation somehow took him aback.

Women usually *did* perform for him, he realised. He only ever saw them at their best—all painted and perfumed and ready for love. He couldn't think of another female who would have worn tights and turned down his offer of another outfit—nor one who would so coolly put the care of her dress before an aroused man. Yet appearances mattered to Aisling, he realised—and part of him reluctantly admired her resolve. Wasn't it one of the reasons why her business had been so successful? Why she had been able to shake off the shackles of her past?

'The wardrobe's through that way,' he said—pointing towards the bedroom at the far end of the corridor and indicating that she should proceed him. Because he wanted to watch her from behind. Wanted to watch the high, taut thrust of her buttocks as they moved against…

'Wait a minute,' he murmured.

'What do you—?' Aisling closed her eyes. 'Gianluca!' she breathed, because he was crouching down to roll down her tights, and kissing the inside of her thighs as he did so. And now he was massaging her ankle with the pad of his thumb and unbuckling her high-heeled shoes. It felt like the most erotic thing which had ever happened to her as he eased the shoes off and put them together neatly, followed by the peeled-off tights, which he placed on top of them. And then he looked up at her, his black eyes glittering, his breath decadently warm against her knees.

'Go and hang your dress up,' he instructed as he stood up.

And Aisling knew that this was all part of the fantasy they were acting out. One night of erotic make-believe which she had agreed to—and she had her own part to play. She couldn't pretend to be some little untutored innocent—even if the dark look of promise in his eyes was making her feel a bit that way.

So she walked down the corridor as unselfconsciously as possible.

'*Lentamente*…slowly,' he commanded huskily as he ran his eyes over her small shoulders, the narrow curvature of her waist—swelling out to the slim bell of her hips. The dark hair fell down her back like a gleaming curtain as she walked with a certain natural grace—yet she did not strut, as a lot of women would if they were being watched by a man.

But when she reached the bedroom, Aisling's stomach began to knot with nerves. It was like something usually featured in one of those brick-sized glossy magazines you found lying around at the hairdressers'—with a bed the size of a soccer pitch and a disconcerting amount of mirrors.

She sensed rather than heard him enter the room behind

her and she forced herself to examine the room as if she were a prospective buyer—anything to buy her time to suppress the debilitating nerves which were suddenly making breathing very difficult.

There was a giant TV screen and electronically controlled blinds, which Gianluca immediately clicked to float down, so that the room was bathed in some surreal, subterranean light.

'Now.' He walked up behind her and lifted the silken curtain of her hair to nuzzle at her neck. 'Are you going to turn around and kiss me?'

She was trembling uncontrollably as she did so, aware that she was almost naked and he was not. 'There's a slightly unfair distribution of clothes around here,' she said.

He laughed. 'Then even it up a little, mmm?'

Her fingers were shaking as she unknotted his silk tie, but he took it from her when she was done and tossed it aside, his black eyes alive with mockery. 'I'll send everything out to the laundry,' he promised. 'Because I don't want to waste precious minutes while you press my suit with your need for neatness and order!'

Was he making fun of her again? But somehow it didn't matter. In fact, nothing mattered apart from what lay ahead. And suddenly Aisling wanted to kick all her usual values into touch—just for that one night. She began to tug at his silk shirt and when a button flew off he gave a low laugh of pleasure—so she tugged even harder and another bounced onto the polished floor.

'Easy, tiger!' he teased.

'But *you're* the tiger!' she retorted, enjoying his instinctive moan as she began to unbuckle his belt. *'Il Tigre.'*

'You've been reading too many press cuttings,' he groaned.

'That's my job.'

'Just shut up about your job for a minute, will you?' he said fiercely.

And now he was unclipping her bra—and his mouth was on her breast and she was bucking with pleasure. She was aware that she was making a mewing sound, like a cat, and that she was inciting him with broken little pleas in between kisses.

And suddenly she could hear the rasping sound of his zip, could feel the formidable power of him springing against her bare skin, and she swayed as he began to push her down to the floor. Now was not the time to tell him that she had never done it on the floor of a luxury penthouse before.

But if he noticed her lack of sophistication, it didn't seem to matter—because he seemed so fired up with excitement that his body was quivering like a tight bow which was stretched to breaking point. He swore again.

'What is it?' she questioned, between kisses.

'I'll have to go and find a damned condom.'

'There's no need. I'm…I'm protected.'

He raised his head. 'But last time—'

Stupid to be shy about the subject of contraception when they were only centimetres away from the ultimate intimacy. 'What happened last time was what galvanised me into going on the pill.' She took a deep breath. There was no need to tell him that she had been scared she wouldn't be able to resist him if ever he tried to seduce her again. *And hadn't she been wise to think that?*

'I see.' He paused for a moment, feeling a complicated mixture of relief that she was prepared for this and yet an intense and inexpicable jealousy at the thought that one day another man might make love to her like this. But that was nothing to do with him. Nothing at all. This was one night and one night only.

She closed her eyes and gasped as he peeled off her panties, his fingers slicking into her honeyed heat as he moved them against the delicate skin in a relentlessly pleasurable rhythm. And then he lifted her up and entered her with one powerful movement and Aisling felt a warm rush as he filled her—so hard and so proud that she sobbed out loud—but everything was happening so quickly.

He was kissing her and moving deep within her, her legs wrapped around his back as she felt the beckoning of her climax and then the first unbelievably powerful wrench as it sucked her under, over and over again—until he made one last, powerful thrust and cried out something in his native tongue.

His head fell onto her shoulder and she could feel the ragged rhythm of his breath and the faint sheen of sweat against her skin and she had to bite back a little cry of sheer wonderment.

How beautiful he was. She wanted to tell him that—and more, too. Crazy, mixed-up thoughts, which were bubbling to the forefront of her mind like a soup, but she held them back. Was that what happened to every woman during lovemaking? she wondered. Was it some sort of evolutionary mechanism which made your feelings for a man crystallise when he had possessed you as thoroughly as Gianluca had just done?

I could quite easily love you, she thought suddenly. She reached out her hands and ran them through the ebony ruffle of his hair, and something in the gesture made him lift his head, his eyes all hooded. This was *Il Tigre* at his most watchful and alert.

'Are you okay?' he queried.

Of all the things he could have said, it was possibly the most inadequate he could have chosen. The kind he might have asked at the end of a long and difficult business meeting. But maybe that was how he regarded it. It was certainly the kind of attitude they'd agreed on before it had all happened. So don't let your stupid feelings show, she told herself. This is one night, no more. 'I'm fine,' she said lightly, her face lighting with a quick smile.

Fine? What kind of a testimony was that? Gianluca surveyed her naked body with the glitter of irritation. Only the rosy bloom which flowered above her breasts gave any indication that she had just been gasping her pleasure in his arms. From the detached expression on her face, you'd think she'd done nothing more exciting than going to the supermarket!

His mouth curved. Let her discover that he had only just begun—and that by the end of the night she would be gazing at him with the rapt adoration he saw as his due. After he had finished with her, she would not regard him so carelessly!

'Let's go to bed,' he said harshly.

CHAPTER EIGHT

DESPITE Aisling's best efforts to preserve the appearance of her pink silk dress, she still felt mortified as she stole down the hotel's grand staircase the following morning.

She had been hoping to get away before anyone was up. Some hopes. Even though it was still early, there were enough people around to notice her and it wouldn't take a genius to work out what she'd been doing. She guessed that a rather creased cocktail dress, spindly stilettos and the remains of last night's make-up might have given the game away. All she prayed was that no client or prospective client was hanging around in this high-profile place to catch her out.

She tried telling herself that she was a grown-up woman in an age of independence where women were equal to men, and why shouldn't she have had a night of consenting passion with a man who happened to be a guest there? But somehow it didn't seem to make much difference to the way she felt.

Did she imagine the raised eyebrows from the more sedately dressed couples going in to breakfast—or the knowing smirks of the reception staff? It was all faintly seedy—and she began to wish that she hadn't resolutely refused Gianluca's offer to help her find a taxi.

But she had wanted to get away from him as soon as was humanly decent—afraid that she would make a fool of herself by telling him that he had been the lover of a lifetime and she wished that it were going to be more than just one night. Because when she'd woken up beside him—it had been to an overpowering feeling of amazement, of being utterly dazed. Half in love and smitten by the hard-faced Italian who had been so exceptionally tender during the night.

Had he deliberately gone out of his way to demonstrate his sensual skills? Very probably. Yet surely the way he'd touched her and held her so close to him had meant more than just expert technique? The way he'd cried out her name at the height of his orgasm—had she imagined real emotion there, or had that been wishful thinking on her part? But could he possibly be like that with every woman he went to bed with?

She didn't know. All she did know was that he had been as cool as rainwater when the alarm on her mobile phone had gone off and she had blinked up at the ceiling, becoming aware of her nakedness and the warm body next to hers.

'I'd better get going,' she said—but, deep down, she was praying he would ask her to stay.

'Yes,' he agreed, even though he could feel himself stirring into life once more. But the pact and night was over—they'd already done it enough times to be memorable. Darkness had melted into the pale light of a winter day. It had been a spectacular night and one he would never forget—but attempt to add anything else into the mixture and it would start to become messy and complicated. Let them both file it under pleasure and move on. 'Me, too,' he yawned. 'Unfortunately, I have a breakfast meeting.'

'Where?'

He opened his eyes then, but the dark glint in their depths spoke of no new intimacy born out of their lovemaking. 'Here in the hotel, actually.'

That was the kick-start she'd needed to try to repair her sex-ravaged appearance and she went into one of the bathrooms to emerge wearing her pink dress.

She picked up her discarded shoes. 'Gianluca—'

Gianluca stilled, because he knew that tone in a woman's voice. He had just come out of the shower himself—wearing only a towel knotted at his hips. His olive body was gleaming, tiny droplets of water sparkling against his ebony head and glittering amidst the dark whorls of hair at his chest. So what did she want? A promise that he still respected her?

He flicked her a glance, thinking how un-Aisling-like she looked this morning—all tousled and flushed, with a slight air of being out of control, no matter how cool her eyes and her voice. *'Sì, cara?'*

'You meant what you said yesterday?'

He raised his dark brows. 'I said many things, Aisling—was there one in particular?'

'About...about us still being able to work together—despite last night.'

Peculiarly, he was disappointed—but since when had realism ever deserted him? Why should she want to lose her most valuable client just because he'd spent the night pleasuring her? Hadn't she already shown herself to be an admirably sharp businesswoman?

'Don't you worry about a thing,' he soothed. 'Last night is forgotten. It will never be mentioned again. As far as you and I are concerned, it is business as usual.'

Somehow that had felt like the worst thing he could have possibly said—and Aisling had experienced a weird sensation of alarm as she had made her way down in the elevator and caught a cab to the office.

Thank heavens she kept spare clothes there and arrived before any of the others, and was able to reapply her make-up and to lose the dress and stilettos without having to face any curious eyes. She sought refuge in a crisp cotton shirt and a smooth pencil skirt and a pair of flat suede shoes, which were reassuringly comfortable.

Stepping back from the mirror, she eyed her image with a resolute expression. It had been a wonderful experience and a sensual treat, but now—just as Gianluca had said—she must put it to the back of her mind.

If only it were that easy. She didn't feel right. She felt…odd. As if something had fundamentally changed in her world. She worried that maybe she had sold herself short in some way—by snatching at something with a man who had offered her nothing but fleeting gratification. Had she been too easy—and should she have played harder to get?

If only she could rid herself of the burning ache she felt in her heart and the torturous replaying of things he'd said and done to her during that long, blissful night. She told herself she wasn't in love with him—and, even if she had been, that absence would soon make him fade into his proper place in her memory bank.

She went through the mechanics of work. She hired a decorator to repaint the hall in her apartment and went shopping in Portobello Road for new pictures for the walls. She booked a spring break in Paris and went to the theatre with a man she met at the gym, before deciding that she didn't like him enough to see him again—even though Suzy, who also knew him, thought she was being completely crazy.

But Suzy didn't know the truth about her brief affair with Gianluca, did she? If she did, perhaps she would have echoed one of Aisling's biggest fears—that she didn't think any other man was ever going to be able to match up to him. Ever.

But not quite her greatest fear. That didn't materialise for several weeks.

It started in the same way she guessed it started for a lot of women. She felt off colour—and could no longer face the piece of wholemeal toast with chunky orange marmalade which she always ate at breakfast time. In fact, the one time she tried it she was very nearly sick, but she put that down to the fact that she'd spent most of the previous evening working until late, with a snatched Chinese meal at the end of it.

Then she began to feel dizzy, with spots appearing before her eyes if she stood up too quickly—and she began to wonder if perhaps she wasn't run down, or if she had been doing too much. Weren't those the symptoms of migraine? Maybe she should make an appointment to see the doctor.

It was only when the nausea began to make her retch when she got out of bed in the morning that she realised there was one simple fact she had failed to consider—and at first she simply refused to believe it.

When she looked back on it afterwards, she was amazed

at how dense she could have been. But denial could be a powerful instinct—particularly when it threatened everything you held dear. For the first time in a long time she felt frightened, and more alone than she'd ever been—even as a child when she'd lain trembling beneath the blankets, waiting for her mother to come home.

She was sitting in her office when she thought everyone else had gone home, feeling completely washed out and tired and just working out the quickest way of getting home, when Suzy came in, a deep frown furrowing her brow.

'Do you have a moment?' she asked, shutting the door behind her.

Aisling looked up at her. 'Can't it wait?'

Suzy shook her head. 'No, I'm afraid it can't.'

What now? Aisling was about to tell her to sit down, when she noticed that Suzy had done exactly that. 'So go ahead,' she sighed. 'Shoot.'

Suzy stared at her. 'How long do you think you're going to be able to hide it, Aisling?' she questioned gently.

'Hide what?'

'The fact that you're pregnant.'

And Aisling burst into tears.

She'd never had a scene at work. Never. Not for Aisling had there been the drunken episode at the Christmas party—or the resignation thrown at the boss in a fit of pique. Yet now she sat there at her desk, howling into a sodden tissue like an overwrought teenager, while Suzy shushed her.

'It's not the end of the world, Aisling,' she soothed. 'Women have babies on their own all the time.'

It didn't seem the right time to tell Suzy that she was

wrong. That Aisling's own experience had convinced her that marriage and love and security and the whole package were the only sensible foundation for bringing up children.

'Does he know?' asked Suzy gently.

Aisling bit her lip. 'No. No, he doesn't.'

'Do you think he'll be…pleased?' questioned Suzy delicately.

'I don't want to talk about it.'

'You're going to *have* to talk about it!' There was a pause. 'Who is the father, out of interest? Obviously somebody very discreet—since we've never seen him.' Suzy frowned. 'He's not married, is he?'

'No, he's not married.'

'Then why all the secrecy?'

Aisling twisted her fingers together, the need to tell someone building inside her, like a pent-up dam which was bursting to break free. 'You won't tell anyone?'

Suzy's eyes narrowed. 'Not if you don't want me to.'

'I don't.' Aisling buried her face in her hands. 'It's Gianluca,' she said, her words muffled.

There was utter silence. 'I beg your pardon?' asked Suzy eventually—in a voice which sounded almost frozen with disbelief.

Aisling looked up as tears began to spill through her fingers. 'It's Gianluca,' she repeated hoarsely.

'Not…not Gianluca Palladio?'

Was there more than one Gianluca in this corner of West London? wondered Aisling slightly hysterically. 'Yes,' she answered dully. 'The very same.'

'Gianluca Palladio—our most illustrious client? The billionaire financier with a penchant for nubile actresses?

The man who once gave a famous interview saying that he wouldn't settle down and marry until he was forty? And that's *six years away*, Aisling!'

Aisling winced. Did Suzy really have to rub salt into the wound? 'Yes. And yes! Oh, Suzy!'

'For heaven's sake, Aisling—what were you *thinking* of? And how long has this been going on?' Suzy shook her short-bobbed head. 'I can't believe I didn't notice.'

In a way, this was even worse, but Aisling couldn't face telling Suzy that the reason she hadn't noticed was because there was, in fact, nothing *to* notice—and that nothing had ever really begun. It had just been a bizarre pact fuelled by nothing deeper than a mutual desire. Viewed now with a dispassionate eye in the cold light of day—it seemed that she must have temporarily taken leave of her senses.

'How pregnant are you?' Suzy's voice broke into her thoughts.

'I don't know.'

'You haven't seen a doctor?'

Aisling shook her head.

Suzy stood up and went and put her arms around Aisling's stiff shoulders. 'Well, that's the first thing you need to do—to find out for sure.'

Was this helpless mass of conflicting emotions really *her*—Aisling Armstrong—or had some weepy impostor taken over her body? 'And the second?' she questioned weakly.

'You'll have to think about telling Gianluca.'

But just *what* was she going to tell him? That she was carrying his child—she who had been nothing but the briefest of flings in his busy life?

And *when* was she going to tell him? Now? When the little baby inside her was little more than a fast-growing bunch of cells, hidden by a gym-flat stomach? Or when those cells had begun to take on an undeniably human form—when she could show him the first amazing black and white photo of the thumb-sucking infant in her womb?

Those thoughts brought her up short. She could accept the pregnancy, yes—the pragmatic side of her knew that was what nature had designed her body for. But a *baby*?

'It's over, Suzy,' she said.

'I guessed that.' Suzy's voice was soft.

'And how the hell am I going to manage to work?' Aisling asked, suddenly scared.

Suzy frowned. 'You're putting the cart before the horse, Aisling. First, you've got to get yourself checked out, and then you've got to tell Gianluca. Work is the least of your worries right now.'

It was so easy to put off something you were dreading—like failing to revise before an important exam and hoping you'd get by on memory and luck. The doctor posed no problem—that was the easy part. He told her that she was in splendid health—and the only thing which made him frown was her workload.

'You've got to cut back a bit on your schedule,' he insisted. 'I know how you modern women like to take everything in their stride—but you mustn't forget that you're growing another human being inside you.'

A human being who bore Gianluca's genes. His dark, mocking face swam into her memory as the reality hit her like a cushioned blow. Aisling went to the coffee bar next door to the office and stared at the flattening clouds of froth on the top of her cappuccino.

So what did she do?

Just *how* did she tell him?

She wasn't due to see him until after she'd found him a new general manager for his new hotel—but as the purchase hadn't gone through she didn't have a clue when that would be. It could be months. She thought about ringing him up—trying to imagine how she'd tell him she was having his baby—but some protective instinct made her want to shy away from the potential of his angry words raining down the phone-line. And over her.

In the end it seemed easier to do nothing. To let the baby grow inside her while she existed in the curiously detached state of well-being which seemed to have descended upon her, like a comforting cloud. It was as if she'd been given an important project to work on—and, being Aisling, she threw herself into it wholeheartedly.

As the weeks slid inexorably into months, she read every book on pregnancy which her local store had to offer. Her diet had always been healthy, but she went for it in a big way—and discovered a deep love of spinach. Once the morning sickness had passed, she found she had an amazing amount of energy, and so she swam at her gym before work, the gentle exercise calming her for the day ahead. It was as though she were living in her own little private bubble of a world—where outside forces had no place.

Only Suzy acted as the voice of her conscience. 'Aisling—this is crazy. You're ballooning by the day. You've *got* to tell him!'

'And I will.'

'When?'

'I don't know. When it's the right time.'

'But time's running out!' cried Suzy, eying the bump with a mixture of fascination and alarm. 'You'll be thinking about giving up work soon.'

Aisling stared down at her stomach as if it belonged to someone else and then gripped the desk with her hands, as if to steady herself. Not only had her body taken on a life of its own, but so had her emotions, and as the weeks passed they grew stronger and stronger. Night after night, she lay in bed while the face of her baby's father swam into her mind's eye and some deep yearning filled her with an inexplicable kind of sadness. 'Some women work until they go into labour,' she said hoarsely.

'But it isn't mandatory,' said Suzy. 'Anyway—that's something we ought to talk about, too. How long you're going to take as maternity leave—or whether you're planning to give up work altogether.'

And that was what freaked Aisling out and brought her crashing to her senses. The sudden dawning that her life was about to change irrevocably—that everything she had strived for could be lost by this unplanned pregnancy. And that she hadn't got into this predicament on her own.

The feeling which had been building and building inside finally burst out and she knew an overwhelming need to tell Gianluca. To connect. To let him know the momentous thing which was about to happen—no matter what had gone on between the two of them.

She looked at the calendar which hung by the little window in her kitchen and stared at the date ringed on it as if someone had crept in while she'd been sleeping and drawn it there. It couldn't really be August, could it? She couldn't really be due to give birth in a fortnight? What if the baby came early—before she had told him?

With a sudden sense of urgency, she lifted the phone and punched out the number of his office in Rome—although she had to speak to three different people before she got through to the great man himself.

'Aisling,' he murmured. 'This *is* a surprise.'

But his voice sounded remote. Wary. As if he was trying to second-guess why she was ringing him—something which he had clearly not been expecting and definitely hadn't wanted, by the sound of it. They both knew there were no outstanding contracts to be discussed—maybe he thought she was contacting him in a transparent attempt to get him into bed again? Aisling shuddered.

'I'd like to see you, Gianluca.'

'Really? Want to tell me why?'

'There's something I need to discuss with you.'

'Go ahead—I'm free now.'

Aisling flinched. He couldn't have made it more plain that he was no longer interested in her. She was past tense and he wanted her to understand that. But a sense of duty and of indignation and some biological imperative to share this with her baby's father drove her on. 'I'd rather not talk about it on the phone.'

'Now I'm intrigued.'

Aisling ignored that. 'Are you coming over to England at all?'

'Regrettably not,' he purred. 'I'm pretty tied up here at the moment. Perhaps you've read that I've just bought a football stadium and it's keeping me pretty busy?'

'Yes,' said Aisling tightly. Who could have forgotten her appalled shock when she'd seen the photograph in the international section of her business paper which had shown Gianluca laughingly surrounded by a posse of scantily clad cheerleaders?

In his office, Gianluca looked out onto the monument of Vittorio Emanuele as it gleamed brilliantly white in the sun, remembering Aisling staring out at it and him inviting her to his vineyard, that first night he'd slept with her. Yet there had only been two nights—and both times it had been the most fantastic sex. She was an interesting woman, there was no denying that. She hadn't pestered him for more—she had kept to their pact, and, undeniably, his opinion of her had gone up as a consequence.

So did this phone call mean that she was hungering for a little more of the pleasure they'd shared?

And wasn't he?

'You miss me?' he questioned.

If the situation hadn't been so deadly serious, Aisling might almost have laughed at his arrogance. 'That's not why I'm ringing.'

'Then just why *are* you ringing?' he questioned coolly.

It was not something she had planned to say over the telephone—but what choice did she have?

'I'm pregnant, Gianluca. With your child.'

There was a silence so long, that for a moment Aisling thought that the connection might have been broken, but as soon as she heard his harsh, cold voice she knew she had been wrong.

'What's your address?' he demanded.

'W-why?'

'Why do you think?' he demanded furiously. 'I'm on my way!'

CHAPTER NINE

GIANLUCA was angry when the plane touched down at the private airfield outside London and even angrier when his car became snarled in a jam outside the capital.

'Can't you hurry it up?' he demanded.

The chauffeur shot a quick glance in his mirror. 'I can try, sir.'

To give the man his credit, he did. They passed the river and then row upon row of narrow streets, crammed with houses which looked tiny to Gianluca's eyes.

'We're here, sir.'

'Pull up a little way back,' Gianluca instructed—because instinct made him want to see her before she saw him. As the car pulled to a halt in front of a tall house, not far from the tube station, Gianluca sat there—brooding and waiting.

How things could change, he thought—and how quickly.

Earlier that day, he had risen from his bed and showered, slid into one of his immaculate suits and drunk some coffee. He had been excited about a new merger—but even more excited about setting up a school sports programme which was to be affiliated with the new football stadium.

Before his breakfast had even been completed he had

arranged to buy a new helicopter and refused the opportunity to take part in a forthcoming television series about successful tycoons. Overall, his feeling as he had been driven to work had been one of a quietly underlying sense of satisfaction. The world according to Gianluca.

And then had come Aisling's phone call.

Apparently he was going to be a father!

Cancelling all his meetings, he had made a few calls before immediately arranging a plane to take him to England. During the flight and the drive from the airport, his thoughts had spun round and round in an unchanging circle as he tried to work out the approximate date of the last time he'd slept with her. Because if she was telling the truth and he was the father of her child as she had implied—then *the baby must be due any time soon*!

He stared out at the tree-lined road. It was the most beautiful English summer's evening—with the intense green leaves of the trees almost blocking out the bright blue of the sky above. Sunlight dappled through the available space, making bright, unmoving patterns on the dusty pavement—for there was not a trace of wind.

But Gianluca found himself looking at it with a highly critical eye. This place was pleasant enough, yes—but it was surrounded by the rest of the city with its noise and crowds and potential dangers. Was this where she planned to bring up the baby? In a culture so alien to his own? And was she intending to give him any say in the matter?

And then he saw a woman walking down the road, walking slowly and rather awkwardly as if the weight of the bags she carried and the heat of the late afternoon were proving too much.

His eyes narrowed and for a moment he didn't recognise her, even though the jacket of her pale summer suit had been cut cleverly in an attempt to conceal her pregnancy. But there was no tailor in the world—no matter how talented—who could disguise the tell-tale signs of impending birth and Gianluca stared at her incredulously as she grew closer.

Madonna mia—but this could not be Aisling!

Narrowing his eyes, he realised he hadn't thought of the baby in real terms—his head had known the facts, but his heart had refused to accept them. He must have slept with her last…last November. He knew that. But time passed and you barely noticed it. That was how lives went by.

Yet this…

He swallowed.

This was a physical manifestation of time passing—because Aisling looked as if she could give birth at any moment!

For a moment, a dark tide of fury washed over him as he acknowledged that she had kept him out of the loop right until the very end. How dared she? How *dared* she?

His heart was pounding but he sucked in a deep breath because instinct told him that he must tread very carefully. That he needed to know what her game was. If ever there was a time when he needed his ability to think logically, it was now.

He let her walk right past.

She didn't notice the car. Didn't stop to glance at the shadowed figure sitting statue-still in the back seat. He could see the faint beads of sweat on her pale forehead and watched while she walked up to her front door and put the carrier bags down, briefly searching around inside her handbag before pulling out a set of keys.

He waited until the front door had shut behind her. Like a tiger who forced himself to linger despite knowing that his prey lay waiting, Gianluca made himself stay in the car for a full five minutes. And then he stepped out.

'Wait here,' he told the driver.

'Any idea how long you might be, sir?'

'None,' Gianluca clipped out and walked up to the door.

It was clearly an apartment—for there were several bells—and he jammed his thumb on the one which said 'A. Armstrong'. And then he remembered her telling him that she lived in a *one-bedded* apartment!

Her voice—sounding disembodied—floated out from the intercom. 'Hello?'

'Hello, Aisling,' he said silkily.

In her stuffy apartment, Aisling's knees went weak and she slumped against the wall, and that was just pure physical reaction to the sound of his deeply sonorous voice. She had known he would come, yes—of course she had—and yet the reality of his impending presence was like a fierce body-blow.

'Gianluca?' she said uncertainly.

'Just open the door, Aisling.'

At least his quietly furious voice gave her some clue what to expect. Weakly, she lifted her hand to buzz him in, when that horrible tight sensation in her back which had been plaguing her since yesterday caught her off guard, and she hesitated.

'Open the door!'

Sucking in a deep breath to try to ease the spasm, she

pressed the entry button and then went to stand beside the French windows she'd just opened—as if trying to put as much space between them as possible.

Stay calm, she told herself. *Just stay calm.*

But that was easier said than done. Her heart was pounding so rapidly and so loudly that she was worried about the baby. The *baby*. She felt the hot shudder of her breath as the tightening in her back increased. Why the hell was she getting *back pain* at a time like this? Hearing the sound of his approaching footsteps, she turned to look out at the garden, not wanting to see his face. Not daring to.

Why, Aisling? Frightened you'll give yourself away—let him know that you can't get him out of your head, and now he's embedded his seed in your body, too.

Shutting the door with a click which sounded like a gun hammer being cocked, Gianluca stopped and stared at her for one long moment. From the back she looked no different. Just a tall, slim woman in a linen skirt and silk shirt, her dark hair caught up in a chignon—though, unusually, a couple of strands of it had escaped and were clinging damply to the back of her long neck.

'Turn around,' he said, and then when she didn't he spoke again. 'I said, turn around and look at me, Aisling.'

Slowly, she complied and Gianluca sucked in a disbelieving breath as he stared at the ripe swell of the unborn child. Even out on the pavement it hadn't seemed quite real. She could have been one of the many passers-by who played their walk-on parts in everyday life—but up here there was no denying it. The evidence was here—as large as life itself.

'What the hell have you *done*?'

In a way his livid eyes and furious voice helped. At least it told her what she had suspected—that Gianluca would want nothing to do with this baby. Yet Aisling had been too independent for too long not to bristle at the unfairness of his accusation. And wasn't justifiable anger a stronger emotion for *her* to hide behind? Wouldn't that prevent her from doing something regrettable like sinking to the floor and begging him to take care of them both?

'What have *I* done?' she demanded. 'Shouldn't that be what have *we* done? Surely you know that it takes two to make a baby!'

'But *which* two?' he lashed out.

Aisling blinked at him uncomprehendingly. 'I'm sorry?'

'There must have been others! Other men? How many others, Aisling?' The white-hot heat of fury that he was going to be a father and that *she hadn't told him* now manifested itself in angry accusation. 'How do I know it's mine?' he demanded.

Did he really think so little of her that she could pretend about something as monumental as *that?* Well, she certainly wasn't going to grovel in order to try to prove herself. 'Do you imagine that I would attempt to foist a false paternity claim on you? What would be the point of that?' she iced back. 'Take a damned DNA test if you don't believe me!'

He stared her out, believing her—her defiance telling him that she spoke the truth. She was a strong woman, yes, but no woman would have been able to maintain such a huge lie about something like this—not in the face of his formidable line of questioning.

'You told me you were protected,' he said quietly.

How *humiliating* it felt to discuss it so cold-bloodedly.

Like picking over the debris after a wild party when everyone else had gone home. 'And I was.'

'So what happened?'

'I had taken antibiotics and they reacted against the pill. I didn't realise. It was an accident, Gianluca.'

'I see. How convenient.'

'Really?' Her head jerked up. 'Convenient for whom? What are you suggesting—that I became pregnant in order to trap you?'

He didn't answer that, just continued to fix her in the ebony spotlight of his eyes, because at the moment he needed facts before reasons. 'When is it due?'

Aisling swallowed down the bitter taste of fear in her mouth. 'Any day now,' she whispered, and the answering light of comprehension which flashed in his black eyes made him look oddly vulnerable and she felt her heart twist with sudden longing. And you stop that right now, she told herself fiercely. He's about as vulnerable as a steel trap.

Any day now. Any day now and his child would be born. Gianluca shook his head as he took in the enormity of this news. She was glaring at him like an adversary, and her attitude made him want to…

He let out a heavy sigh. To what? He didn't know. But he could see that her skin was paler than perhaps it should have been—the beads of sweat about more than a stuffy summer's day—and he was stricken with a momentary guilt.

'Hadn't we better sit down?' he suggested. 'You in particular.'

Proudly, Aisling drew her shoulders back, then winced as the nagging pain in her back began to grow more intense. 'I don't remember inviting you to stay.'

'Sit down!' he urged urgently.

Aisling did as he said, suddenly realising just how tense she was and as her hand fluttered instinctively over her bump she saw his eyes drawn to it with an expression of horrified fascination.

'You need a drink,' he said grimly. And so did he.

Pointing wordlessly towards the kitchen, she didn't contradict him. She needed something. Anything. She felt faint. Sick—and she didn't want to harm the baby.

It wasn't a huge apartment and the doors along the corridor on the way to the kitchen had been left open. All bar one. He passed a gleaming white bathroom and, right beside it, a closed door.

He knew he shouldn't open it. That this was her place and it wasn't his right to do so. Yet what Gianluca had learnt had turned his whole world upside down. Did she have the monopoly on secrets? Did she control all the information which flowed in and out of his life? Like hell she did!

Quietly, he turned the door handle and just stood there, as if he had been carved from rock. For this was Aisling's bedroom, yes—with its big bed and its neat counterpane. And off the bedroom was what must have once been a dressing room and which she was now clearly intending to act as a nursery. Silently, he walked towards it and it was as alien to his life as if a meteor had crashed in through the ceiling and embedded itself on the soft, primrose-coloured carpet.

She must have spent years wanting and waiting for this baby, he thought—because the tiny room was furnished with loving care and precision to detail. Yellow seemed to be the main colour. Did that mean she didn't yet know the sex—or was that something *else* she was withholding from him?

There was an old-fashioned crib draped with gauzy material, which had some kind of gold thread running through it—making it look like a canopy of sunshine. There was a mobile hanging over it, composed of different animals—both wild and domestic—and Gianluca's mouth curved as his fingers drifted over the sleek body of a tiger.

Quietly, he shut the door and his eyes were hooded when he returned to the sitting room a couple of minutes later, with a beaker of iced water for her and a glass of wine for himself. She took the tumbler from him with shaking fingers and gulped some down, spilling a little as she did—so that drops of it splashed over the material which strained over her bump.

But he didn't sit down, he just drank off half a glass of wine with a speed he'd never used before and stood staring down at her. 'Why didn't you tell me sooner?' he demanded.

Why, indeed? Because she was frightened of his reaction? And hadn't she been right to be—judging by the thunderous look on his face? 'There never seemed to be a right time,' she said.

'So you wait until now—when it is almost over,' he said bitterly.

She looked at him. 'Over? It hasn't even begun, Gianluca.'

'Madre di Dio!' he exclaimed, in a strangled voice as the monumental significance of what had happened really hit home and he half wanted to turn his back and to walk away from her—to erase her and this unplanned baby from his life. Yet there was part of him which wanted to go over to her, to take away her hand and to lie his own over her belly—perhaps to feel the infant kick beneath him.

He took another swallow of his wine and looked away.

He must keep focussed and deal with the facts, he reminded himself. Then, and only then, would he be able to decide what action to take.

'You planned this?' The accusation cracked out like a pistol shot.

'Planned it?' Aisling looked up at him in confusion and then realised what he meant. 'You think…you think I got pregnant on purpose?'

'Did you?'

She balled her hands into two tiny fists, wanting to scream and shout and flail, but recognised that all these were indulgences she could ill afford—and especially not at a time like this. This was Gianluca she was dealing with. *Il Tigre* at his most calculated even though his bitter words were coated in anger. She needed to keep all her wits about her—because if there was one thing she could count on, it was that Gianluca was going to be keeping his.

'No. I didn't get pregnant on purpose. Why would I do something like that?'

He gave a mirthless laugh. 'Oh, come on! Use your imagination, *cara*. I happen to know you have a very good one. Any woman having a child of mine would be set up for life!'

Even in the midst of her disquiet such an audacious piece of chauvinism made her blink. 'That's rather an extreme method of guaranteeing financial security, isn't it?' she questioned drily.

She saw his eyes narrow in surprise and suddenly knew that this was the way to go. She *needed* to stand up to him. She must *not* go to pieces. Because he was a powerful man—he exuded influence and authority from every fibre. She could feel it radiating from his spectacular body as he stood there, darkly intimidating—an interloper in her home. And yet she carried that interloper's child inside her. Biologically, at least, she was tied to this man for life.

'Well, you needn't worry on that account, Gianluca—I'm not asking you for anything.'

'Then why did you bother telling me?' he flashed out.

'Because—strange as it may seem— I felt that, as the father, you had a right to know.' Aisling put her empty glass down with a thud. 'But now I've done the right thing, you can forget all about it. I can see from your face that this is unwanted—so why don't you just go away and leave me alone?'

'Go away?' he echoed in disbelief. 'Are you out of your mind, *cara mia*? Is that really what you imagine I would do?'

Suddenly she didn't know. Tiredly, she shook her head—hating the heavy weight of her hair and thinking that if she had a nearby pair of scissors she would lop the whole lot off.

'Didn't you think through what the repercussions of telling me might be?' he persisted.

It was a horrible word and she stared at him, hoping that she hid her alarm. 'What do you mean—repercussions?'

'You carry my child!' he breathed fiercely. 'You cannot deny me that child—and, what is more, I will not let you!'

For a moment Aisling stared at him in horror, the look of intent on his dark face so threatening that he looked almost capable of carrying her away with him. Why the hell had she told him? The pain in her back now seemed to be gaining momentum, spreading round to spear at her abdomen, but she choked back the little cry of pain which was gathering at the back of her throat.

'Look, Gianluca, this was never meant to happen,' she said desperately.

'You mean you wish it hadn't?' he demanded.

Afterwards Aisling would wish that she had thought more carefully about answering that particular question, but her head was swimming and another sharp twist of pain was piercing at her middle and she just wanted everything to be as it was before. No discord. Just that fluffy pink cloud which had stopped her thinking about an unthinkable future. One which involved a baby.

'Do you, Aisling? You wish it hadn't happened?'

'Of course I do!' she burst out, in the grip of some terrible hormonal rush. All those old childhood insecurities came rushing back in a terrifying dark wave which was threatening to swamp her. 'Don't you think this threatens everything I stand for, everything I've worked for?'

There was a deadly silence and when he looked at her the expression in his eyes had changed. Even their colour looked different. Suddenly black seemed like the coldest colour in the world.

'Then there's no problem. We won't let it affect you,' he said icily.

Aisling's nails dug into the palm of her hand. 'What are you talking about?'

'None of this need affect anything,' he chipped out. 'You can keep your precious job and everything which goes with it—and I will keep the baby. A perfect solution to an unwanted pregnancy.'

All she could see was the narrowed jet eyes, the lips curled with cruel intent—like a tiger about to attack. She might have protested—answered him back—but by then his words seemed as inconsequential as whether or not it remained sunny outside. Because now there was no world outside—it was all in here. Here and now. The pain was twisting sharper—as if someone were turning a meat skewer inside her—and she gasped and tumbled forward, the weight of the baby seeming to make her topple, like a giant clown.

She saw Gianluca start and then it was as if everything were happening in slow motion—so that while she sensed he was rushing to her side, he seemed to be moving through water. But maybe that was because all the external things seemed blurred—put out of focus by the intensity of what was happening inside her.

He caught her in his arms before she fell—the warm and unfamiliarly heavy weight of her—and he carried her over to a sofa and laid her down on it, his eyes scanning over her, fearful of what he might see.

'What is it, Aisling? What is happening? Tell me. *Tell* me!'

She had no idea, and yet she knew—as women must have known since they'd lived in caves.

'I'm having a...baby!' she gasped. 'Just call me an ambulance, will you?'

'There's no need for an ambulance,' he grated as he bent down and scooped her up into his arms. 'My car's outside.'

'I'm booked in at the local hospital down the road,' she gasped.

'Not any more you're not—I'll get you into the best clinic in London,' he snapped.

Even through her pain, Aisling felt a wave of indignation. 'It's a fantastic hospital,' she gritted out. 'And I'm going there. Besides, there's no time for messing around.'

He raked his eyes over her and recognised that she spoke the truth. 'Where are your keys?'

'On the hook,' she gasped as he plucked them off and pocketed them and proceeded to carry her towards the car. Her face was pressed against his chest, the scent of him invading her—as if one invasion of her wasn't enough. Moving her head away, she half-heartedly tried to pummel against him, but his chest was as solid as a brick wall. 'Put me down!'

'Save your energy, Aisling,' he urged, his face and his voice becoming suddenly serious. 'I demand that you conserve your strength—because you are going to need it!'

To the chauffeur's credit he said nothing when Gianluca emerged from the villa with a heavily pregnant woman in his arms—just leapt out of the driver's seat and pulled the door open.

Gianluca settled Aisling in the back seat and gave the driver the address. 'Drive!' he commanded. 'Quickly—but *lievemente*—gently.' He saw the man shoot them an anxious glance and who could blame him? Because Aisling was now moaning every few minutes, her face tightening with tension as she gripped onto him.

'Is it the contraction?' he demanded.

'Of course it's the wretched contraction!' she half sobbed. 'What else do you think it is?'

'Do you want me to call anyone for you?' He realised how little he knew about her—this woman who carried his child. 'Your mother?'

'My mother is dead.'

He winced. 'You have any other family?'

As the fierce wave of pain receded Aisling briefly opened her eyes. 'No. Just me.'

Somehow, that smote at his conscience—that she had done this all on her own, with no one to protect her—until he reminded himself that it had been *her* choice to do it that way.

At least the rush-hour traffic had now died away and the baking city streets were relatively quiet, but he didn't breathe easily until the car bumped its way round the back of the hospital.

'We're here.'

Aisling's eyes flickered open as she read the sign. 'Accident and Emergency. How apt,' she said, her voice cracking. 'The baby was an accident—and this is an emergency!'

Gianluca nearly smiled but for once in his life, he didn't dare—if they didn't get a move on then his son or daughter was going to be born in a car park. But a wheelchair and a doctor and midwife had miraculously materialised out of nowhere and Aisling was being taken at breakneck speed to the maternity unit—and then chaos broke out. Or, at least, that was how it seemed to him.

There were lights and people dressed in green, battering him with questions, most of which he was unable to answer—because she had *kept him in the dark*, he thought, and once again that sense of dark fury washed over him.

'Are you the father?' a midwife asked.

At least he knew the answer to *that* one—though he found himself telling them in his native tongue. *'Sì, io sono il padre!'*

'So you'll be staying?'

Aisling's head jerked up. 'No!'

'*Sì,*' he contradicted with silky emphasis as he stared down into her ice-blue eyes. 'I will be staying.'

She didn't want him there. Didn't want him seeing her in such a vulnerable and sorry state. Now they were putting her legs up in some kind of stirrups—how could she ever look at him again after this? She bit her lip with embarrassment and turned away as the contractions began to get stronger, and more frequent.

And by then she was past caring about anything, other than following what they were telling her to do—or, rather, telling her *not* to do. Like push. Or *bearing down*. And she, who hated control being taken from her, found that she wanted so badly to relieve these tightening bands of pain that she almost welcomed the bossy orders they were hurling at her. She might have laughed at the irony of it all if she hadn't been so exhausted.

The room was crowded for it seemed that the royal obstetrician had been rushed in from his nearby private clinic, following a directive from Gianluca's doctor in Rome.

'Please!' Aisling begged. 'I just want to have this baby!'

Gianluca shot an anxious glance at the doctor, but for once in his life he was forced to relinquish control. He wanted to help Aisling, but he could do nothing for her physically—or emotionally—because when he went to grip her hand, she pulled it away, refusing to look at him.

It was only when he sensed that the labour was close to the end, when her desperate cries echoed on the air, that she reached for him, biting her lip with pain as her fingernails pierced his skin.

'Help me,' she whispered. 'Gianluca—please help me.'

Never in his life had he felt so completely powerless.

'It's going to be all right, *cara*,' he soothed, but his voice sounded harsh.

She turned her sweat-sheened face away. He lied. For how could it ever be right?

'Gianluca, do you want to see your baby being born?'

He turned to Aisling and the moment their eyes met she knew that she could not deny him this. And as she nodded her head with mute permission, she so wished that it could have all been different. Normal. That they could have been like other couples in this situation. *But you aren't a couple*, came the painful reminder, before another, vastly superior pain eclipsed it.

Gianluca was dazed as he watched the physical process of childbirth, which seemed light years away from the desire which had brought them all to this point. One last cry from Aisling split the air. He saw a shock of jet-dark hair emerging and heard a lusty squawk and he shook his head, as if denying the evidence of his own eyes. This miracle.

But when a slimy and wriggling bundle was swathed and placed in his arms, Gianluca looked down, and his heart turned over with love.

CHAPTER TEN

'YOUR partner is waiting to collect you, Aisling.'

'Thanks.' With hands which were trembling slightly, Aisling picked up the baby.

It was pointless correcting the midwife. Let her believe that she and Gianluca were cosy partners if it fitted the happy-ever-after version. The sad truth was that they said very little of any consequence to each other. His soft, murmured words were for his son alone—and his brilliant, charismatic smiles for the nursing and medical staff to whom he was so grateful.

'Fancy him trying to keep that donation to the special care baby unit quiet!' cooed the midwife. 'And theatre tickets for the entire department, too! You're one lucky woman, Aisling.'

Lucky? Aisling's face didn't betray a thing as she adjusted her son's cashmere blanket for the eighth time since she'd draped it around him—wondering where the self-possession on which she prided herself had fled to.

Did other new mothers feel like this? Scared witless that they were going to do something wrong. Worried about dropping the baby—or making him too hot, or too cold.

This beautiful little baby who so resembled his father and was so far unnamed, because neither of them could agree on anything they liked.

She felt all over the place—as if the ground had turned into slippery ice since she gave birth a little over twenty-four hours ago—and everyone knew how to skate on it except her. The midwives had told her that it was early days and part of Aisling had wanted to ask to stay longer—knowing that at least while she was in hospital she didn't have to make any big and troublesome decisions.

But that was not the way that childbirth was conducted any more. New mothers were encouraged to take their babies home as soon as the baby was feeding well so that the family could all 'bond'. Well, she couldn't see that happening in her case.

'Aisling?'

She heard the sound of Gianluca's velvety voice and inside she prayed for some sort of guidance on how best to handle this situation—surely the most bizarre state of affairs imaginable? To maintain some kind of emotional balance and make sure she knew the difference between fact and reality.

She turned round to see his eyes sweep over the sleeping bundle she cradled in her arms—his expression all bright and shine. And then his features became shuttered as he met her gaze. Was he inwardly cursing her for trapping him, despite his obvious joy at the birth of his son? she wondered.

'Are you ready?' he questioned.

She nodded. 'Sure.'

'Shall I carry him?'

'Yes, of course.' Aisling tried to tell herself that it was

only fair he should—and she carefully handed the baby over, hoping that her face did not betray her inner panic. Because, unlike her, Gianluca seemed to be a natural at this. The baby looked like a swaddled white blob—almost lost in those powerful arms, which could be so strangely gentle with the infant.

He ran a questing fingertip over the baby's cheek and murmured something soft in Italian before lifting his head to look at Aisling and switching to English. 'The car is outside. Are you okay to walk?'

'Yes, I'm fine.'

They spoke like strangers—intimate strangers—and the journey back to the flat was punctuated by long silences broken only by the little sucking sounds the baby made. Perhaps Gianluca was as inhibited as she was by the chauffeur's presence—or maybe it was just the confined space and claustrophobic intimacy of the car. All Aisling knew was that when she emerged into the unseasonable drizzle of the summer day she had begun to shiver.

There was no excitement in her heart as they walked into her apartment—the place had a disused and empty feel to it, even though she'd only been away for a little more than a day.

'Shall I put him in his crib?' questioned Gianluca.

She nodded. 'Yes, do. He shouldn't be hungry. I fed him before we left. I'll go and make coffee.'

Not that she wanted coffee and neither, she suspected, did he. But she needed something to occupy her hands and her thoughts—anything to avoid staring across the room at him and wondering where they went from here. Slowly, she slipped off her raincoat and automatically hung it in the hall, then she went to put the kettle on.

It felt weird just doing something as normal as making coffee and she had to force herself to remember the mechanics of it. It was as if the experience of childbirth had detached her from the rest of the world and made her look at it differently. A kettle was no longer just a kettle—overnight it had become a baby-hazard!

When she came back into the sitting room it was to see that Gianluca was back from the nursery and was standing looking down at the rain-washed garden.

Almost guiltily, she ran her eyes over him—as if sexual fantasy were out of bounds now that she had a new role to play as mother.

Today, he was dressed casually and his dark hair was ruffled, and slightly longer than he usually wore it. Aisling swallowed down the salty threat of tears which threatened to prick at the backs of her eyes.

How strange that, despite the icy politeness which had existed like a thick wall between them since she'd gone into labour, her heart could still turn over with longing for the love he would never give her.

With an effort, she fixed her face into a smile. 'Would you like some coffee?' she asked.

He turned round and his mouth hardened. 'What I would like, Aisling,' he responded softly, his black eyes glittering, 'is for us to come to a few decisions.'

She eyed him in alarm. 'Can't this wait?'

'Until when?' he demanded. 'Until he's six months old? A year? Until *you* decide you're ready to talk? But this isn't about you, Aisling—not any more. You kept me out of his life before he was born—but those days are gone. There are three of us now—and you'd better get used to that.'

Three of us. In a way his harsh words mocked at what she most wanted—a secure unit in which to raise her son, the kind of unit she'd never known herself. And now it looked as if that was a legacy she was about to bequeath to the baby—giving him all the insecurities attached to having a single mother. 'What do you want to talk about, Gianluca?'

He registered how washed-out she looked. How her skin seemed almost transparent, and he wondered briefly if she needed more time, but then he steeled his heart against her pale face. *Madonna mia*—but he wasn't asking her to go out and work in the fields! What he wanted wasn't unreasonable—not to his way of thinking.

He let his eyes drift over her. She had woven her hair into two thick plaits, knotted raven ropes which contrasted against her skin, a style which made her appear ridiculously young—much too young to have a baby. But at least that hated chignon was gone!

'His name, for a start.'

Aisling nodded. The name she could cope with. 'Do you have any more suggestions?'

'Do you?' he questioned silkily.

'You still don't like James?'

He shook his head.

'William?'

He laughed. 'I think we both know that I won't be satisfied with any name which isn't Italian, *mia bella*.'

Yes, she knew that. And didn't he have a point? With his jet-black hair and huge, dark eyes, their son would look all wrong with a name like Andrew, or James or William.

'Okay. Fire some suggestions at me.'

'I thought of Claudio.' He studied her reaction. 'It was my father's name—it's strong and I like it. Do you?'

'Claudio.' She tried the name. Closed her eyes and pictured the image of her son—already burned there for the rest of her lifetime. Yes, it suited him. It suited him very well. She opened them again, to find Gianluca watching her—a wary expression on his face, as if he were expecting something unpredictable. So start being yourself again, she reasoned. Stop being this shaky bag of post-partum insecurities. Bring back the woman who can cope with anything life throws at her. 'Yes. I like that.'

'Good.' He poured them both coffee and handed her one and as she moved forward he noticed the swollen heaviness of her breasts and felt the unexpected beat of desire. A sudden yearning to go over there and kiss her.

Did men usually want their women this quickly after birth? he wondered—aware that this was completely new territory to him. Mercilessly, he swamped the feeling—because desire could cloud judgement and he needed his to be crystal-clear right now. 'But this was about more than just a name—we also need to make some pretty big decisions.'

Her senses prickled. 'Such as?'

'Oh, come on, Aisling. There is Claudio's future at stake here. Just out of interest—how do *you* see that future?'

It was strange to hear him say their son's name. As if the baby had suddenly become a real person. And she would have been a fool if she had not anticipated this particular question either. 'I've thought about it a lot and I think we can come to some sort of perfectly amiable agreement.'

He raised his dark brows. How calm she sounded. How utterly in control. 'Really?'

'Yes. I can do bits of work from home for the time being—and then I can go in part-time.'

Gianluca's eyes narrowed in disbelief. 'Aren't you forgetting something in this cosy little scenario?'

Aisling stared at him. 'Such as?'

'Where does my son's welfare come into all this?' he demanded. 'And where do *I* fit in?'

She heard the fiercely possessive note in his voice when he said 'my son' like that and her heart sank. None of this was happening as it was supposed to and Aisling wanted to reassure him—to tell him that she wasn't going to deny him his child, but she wasn't going to crowd him with unrealistic demands, either. She certainly wasn't going to become one of those troublesome ex-girlfriends who was always looming into his life like a spectre, with a baby in tow.

'You know you can see the baby whenever you like!' she protested.

'How very generous of you, *mia cara*,' he replied, with soft sarcasm. 'But aren't you forgetting simple geography?'

Aisling nodded because she had been anticipating this, too. 'Okay—so you live in Italy and I live in London—but the world has shrunk, Gianluca. You know it has. You can see Claudio...' But her words trailed away as he leaned forward, eyes blazing black fire.

'When? A weekend a month? A holiday in the summer? My boy growing up unable to speak Italian? You expect me to tolerate such a situation?' He looked around and made an arrogantly sweeping gesture with his arm. 'And you expect me to stand back and allow you to bring him up somewhere like *this*?'

'What's the matter with it?' she questioned, stung—for she was very proud of her little home. 'There's nothing wrong with where I live!'

'I'm not saying there is—it's fine for a working woman, but not one who has a young child. There's only one bedroom, for a start! Where's he going to crawl when he's able to? Out in that *minuscolo*—tiny little garden? Or straight into the traffic outside?'

'Loads of people bring up children in London!'

'Not my child,' he said flatly. 'Unless you're expecting me to buy you a house? Is that what you are angling for?'

She stared at him, recoiling from the suggestion. 'I won't take your money—not for a house!' she said proudly. 'You can contribute towards his upkeep, if you insist.'

Upkeep. It was such a soulless little word and one which crystallised the idea which had been forming in the back of his mind since she had first told him that she was pregnant. Knowing that it was the only way to guarantee that he would not be pushed to the sidelines, according to her mood or whim.

'I'm going to insist on a lot more than that, *cara*,' he vowed softly.

Aisling sank back against the chair and eyed him warily. 'You won't change my mind. There isn't an alternative.'

He moved in for the kill. 'Oh, but there is.' Gianluca paused for maximum impact, as he always did before making an important announcement.

'Oh?'

'You will marry me,' he said.

'M-marry you?'

'Sì, cara. Mi sposa.'

Just for one mad split-second she allowed her heart to soar. To imagine that he meant it in the way that most proposals of marriage were meant. But the look on his arrogant face spoke of no emotion other than the most fundamental one of possession. Ownership. As he owned hotels and properties. He wanted to own his son and, in order to do so, he must first marry his son's mother.

'It is the only sensible solution,' he drawled.

Aisling swallowed down the hurt. 'You think so?'

'All I know is that marriage will give me equal rights in Claudio's life. Come on, Aisling—surely you, as a practical woman, can see the justice in that?'

Aisling stared at him, knowing she didn't have a leg to stand on. The trouble was that she could see it from Gianluca's point of view. Already, he loved Claudio with a passion she suspected was rare for this powerful man. Did she really have the right to deny him the legal right to participate in his child's life?'

Aisling swallowed. 'But marriage is…'

'Is what? It's practical, for a start—something which should appeal to you, Aisling. It's a legal document. A contract.'

And there she had been—stupidly believing that marriage was about love and romance.

'And two people looking after a baby is easier than one on their own,' he continued softly.

Had he noticed her awkwardness around Claudio, then? Did he think her incapable of being left to care for a baby? But that was a question she dared not ask, and so she stuck to one she did. 'And just where do you propose we live?'

Gianluca narrowed his dark eyes. 'There is only one place for us to live,' he said softly. 'And that is in Italy.'

'Gianluca—'

'You think I will tolerate Claudio being brought up in cramped conditions in London when he can have all the space he needs in rural Umbria—with the freshest air in the world for his little lungs?' he demanded. 'I have a large house in the Umbrian hills with enough staff to provide you both with every comfort you desire.'

'But my independence?' Aisling ventured and saw his mouth twist with derision as she recognised that it was the wrong word to use. She wanted to explain that she felt frightened—as if she were submerging her own identity in a sea of other people's expectations—but she saw the repressive look in his black eyes and knew that he wasn't interested in *her* needs. And why should he be? It was his son and only his son which mattered to Gianluca.

'Is there no other solution?' she asked weakly, realising that her normal strength and resilience had been sapped by birth and circumstances. And didn't the thought of being taken care of for the first time in her life have an appeal she couldn't deny?

'You are on maternity leave,' pointed out Gianluca smoothly. 'So what is there to keep you and Claudio in England right now? You have already told me that you have no family.'

He made her sound as disposable as a paper handkerchief! She stared at him, aware that he seemed to have taken over and yet unable to fault his logic. What *was* keeping her in England, other than pride? And wasn't pride pointless? She knew Gianluca well enough to understand that he would crush her pride underfoot if it interfered with how much he could see his son.

'And, of course, I can arrange for a nanny,' he continued. 'To help you.'

'A nanny?' she repeated dully.

'We'd need a nanny whatever happened,' he said smoothly. 'With two working parents it's inevitable. You do still *want* to work, I assume?'

'Yes, of course,' she answered stiffly.

But Aisling was uncomfortably imagining some fresh-faced beauty looking after their baby. Someone who could supplant her? Who would inevitably fall for her billionaire boss? She felt as if she were in a fog—fighting to see the clear horizon. 'But…but…'

Gianluca raised his brows in autocratic query. 'What is it, Aisling?'

She stared at him before asking the question. The other big one which was nagging away at the back of her mind. 'What *kind* of marriage did you have in mind?'

Their eyes met for a long moment and then his gaze swept over her once more, only this time in a much more leisurely appraisal—as if her words had just given him permission to do so.

It was astonishing how all the weight she had carried along with Claudio seemed to have melted away. Her breasts were heavier, true—but that was no bad thing—and there was a new and irresistible softness about her. Like an ice cream which was beginning to melt, making you want to lick it all up. A nerve flickered at his temple and his voice grew husky.

'I think you know which kind of marriage would work

best—especially as the sex between us is so good. We can thrash out the details later—the important thing is that we agree the contract in principle.'

Especially as the sex is so good?

Thrash out the details later?

Aisling was glad that she was sitting down. He could not have found a more insultingly cold-blooded way of putting it if he had tried. Yet wasn't he only doing what she had attempted to do for most of her life until she'd met him? To keep messy emotion at bay?

The trouble was that her heart had somehow become involved along the way. It still was. And now that they shared a child—there would never be any real peace, nor escape from him and this terrible aching deep inside her. She might bear his name as she had borne his child, but his love would never be hers. 'And what if I won't marry you?'

Gianluca's eyes narrowed, for he did not underestimate her—though surely she must recognise that she was in no position to bargain with him? She was an intelligent woman, *sì*—but she did not have his resources. And neither did she have this terrible fear that if his son was taken from his life, then his heart might as well be ripped from his chest. For a man the world perceived as having everything, Gianluca realised that unless he had Claudio, he had nothing.

'Then I will fight you in the courts,' he vowed softly. 'However long and however much it takes—I will fight you for custody, *cara*. And I will win, Aisling—because I always do.'

'Then there is nothing left to say, is there?' she asked him quietly. 'Yes, I will marry you. There. You have your victory, Gianluca.'

His eyes narrowed as she bit her lip and turned her head away and a brief but unexpected thought flew into his mind.

That if victory it was—it suddenly seemed a rather hollow one.

CHAPTER ELEVEN

THE marriage took place in a small, hillside church in Umbria—not far from Gianluca's vineyard home.

It was an odd kind of wedding, attended only by a handful of guests—Gianluca's old nanny, his lawyer and the town mayor. Aisling had wanted to treat the occasion as a mere formality and wear something smart from her existing wardrobe—as if not making a fuss might protect her from the emotional fallout of marrying a man who did not love her.

But Suzy had persuaded her otherwise, in spite of her own disappointment at not being invited because Aisling had told her fiercely that it was only a marriage of *convenience*. A legal formality and nothing more—done for Claudio and no other reason.

'Even if it is all that—it's a celebration,' Suzy insisted. 'You can't just treat it like any other day.'

'He doesn't love me.'

'But you love him, don't you?'

Aisling's eyes filled with tears. Oh, yes. More than she had thought possible. 'Of course I love him,' she whispered. 'It's crazy, but I do. And it's a million times stronger since I gave birth to his son.' Furiously, she dabbed at her eyes with a small fist. 'He thinks I got pregnant to trap him.'

'You didn't, did you?'

'Of course I didn't!' Aisling wailed. 'But if you can think it—no wonder he does!'

Suzy shook her head. 'None of this is relevant, Aisling,' she said softly. 'All that matters is that you have a baby between you and the marriage *is* going ahead. You've got to make the best of it—for Claudio's sake, if nothing else. Look on it as a celebration of *him*, of this brand-new life you've created. Make him be proud of his mother when he looks back at the wedding photos!'

And it was those words which struck a chord and stirred Aisling into action. Didn't she owe it to Claudio to make the most of what circumstances had thrown at her?

So she bought a simple ivory-coloured silk dress—even though she had been tempted to go for something in a colour she usually wore, so that she could wear it again afterwards. Practical, as always.

But she was spurred on by a crazy yet irresistible hunger to *feel* like a bride, even if it was only a role she had been forced to play by circumstance. And as it was probably the only time she was ever going to do it, she ended up buying everything—matching shoes, handbag, even pale stockings and lacy lingerie which was a million miles away from the underwear she usually sported.

Two days before they left for Italy, she stopped outside an upmarket baby boutique and, on impulse, went inside. She found what she hadn't realised she'd been looking for—the sweetest little white sailor-suit in the lightest lawn-cotton. It even had a jaunty matching hat and tiny bootees and it would be perfect for the wedding.

And when Gianluca's elderly nanny exclaimed her approval before the service started, Aisling knew she had made the right decision to act the part. Because that was all it was—play-acting.

Yet Gianluca looked so tall and impossibly handsome that Aisling felt her heart swelling with love and pride as she repeated the marriage vows. Her hand was shaking as she signed the register and she could feel the heat from his body as he leaned over her—the sheer masculine scent of him invading her senses and making her long to feel him in her arms again. How long had it been since they'd had sex? Well, that wasn't difficult to remember—not since the night their son was conceived!

This close she could see his golden-olive skin and the thick black hair—and that amazingly autocratic profile. He turned his head to look at her and Aisling swallowed down her longing. How sensual his lips looked today, she thought. It seemed for ever since those lips had kissed her, had explored every single part of her body in a way which could still make her yearn for it to happen all over again.

Gianluca had booked a late lunch at an amazing restaurant run by a friend of his in the next town—and Aisling was surprised to see that the table was decorated with balloons and fresh flowers. At the end of the meal they even brought out the traditional Italian wedding cake of a *Mille Foglie*—a light and dreamy concoction topped with a smiling plastic bride and groom.

'I wasn't expecting this kind of…fuss,' she said to

Gianluca in a low voice, not sure how well she was keeping up the masquerade of supposedly happy bride.

'Weren't you?' He thought how unlike most women she really was. That she had refused his offer of the biggest engagement ring the shop had to offer, saying that she didn't think such a gesture would be 'appropriate'. She might be ice-cold, but she certainly wasn't mercenary. His ran his gaze over her—from the top of her fragrant hair to the high heels of some very sexy shoes. Was she sending out a message? he wondered idly. A silent invitation that she was prepared to break this unendurable tension between them, in the only way which would?

'And by the way, you look utterly *delizioso*,' he murmured. '*Sensuale*. Like the *Mille Foglie*—you look good enough to eat, and I should like to do just that right now.'

Aisling felt a blush spreading from her face all the way down to her suddenly tingling breasts—and she felt horribly vulnerable. Wasn't this day difficult enough, without her going to pieces just because he had implied…? 'Gianluca—'

'Gianluca, *what*?' he mocked. 'Please don't bring up the one subject which has been preoccupying both of us.'

She shot a hot-faced glance at Fedele, although the lawyer appeared to be engrossed in conversation with the owner of the restaurant. 'Please. Not in front of the others,' she whispered.

He bent his head closer—close enough to remind her of how it had felt to have his lips on her and his body deep in hers. 'Don't you think it's normal for a bride and groom to think about sex on their wedding day, *mia bella*?'

Perhaps if he had used another word other than *sex*,

then Aisling might have responded with a degree of enthusiasm—or was she just fooling herself? Wasn't there a part of her which welcomed his cold-blooded description—as if that would reinforce the fact that this marriage existed solely as a *contract* and not a true marriage at all. Should she condemn his lack of diplomacy—or commend him for his honesty?

Aisling jabbed her fork into the wedding cake, but failed to lift it to her mouth. And wasn't the whole point that she *did* want him? Wouldn't she be crazy to deny herself the physical pleasure of his body just because she couldn't have his love? And surely it would make the already-existing tension between them unendurable if she did.

After the meal ended, he drove the three of them back to the vineyard and Aisling told herself she was glad that the baby's presence ruled out anything as traditional as being carried over the threshold. Come to think of it, she wasn't even sure whether it *was* a tradition in Italy—and it did not seem appropriate to ask.

But Gianluca's eyes narrowed as the door closed behind him, observing the tiredness which had given her such a strained look.

'Why don't you go and take a bath?' he suggested softly. 'And just relax. It's been a long day.'

The unexpected kindness in his voice made her turn away before he could see the prick of tears in her eyes. 'Yes. I think I will.'

Gianluca had rearranged the upstairs of the house, so that a whole floor of rooms had been arranged for them, with a nursery suite for Claudio. Which meant that she and her new husband could sleep alone, or together…

After changing out of her bridal finery, Aisling ran a bath and had a long and luxurious soak, but even though the tension was seeping from her body her mind wouldn't stop racing. She lay there, watching all the bubbles gradually dissolve—and wondering where the hell they went from here. It was as if their energy had been focussed on the trip to Italy and the wedding—and now just the great unknown waited.

She slipped into some cool linen trousers and a shirt which made breast-feeding easier. Then she tied her hair back into a pony-tail before going downstairs to look for them.

It was strange, navigating this house where Gianluca had grown up but which was so new and so alien to her. So much of living was instinctive, she thought—like the way she still turned left out of the bathroom as if she were in her old flat, instead of in this huge place. Would she ever grow used to it—and would it ever feel like home?

She found Gianluca and Claudio in the garden which overlooked the glitter of the distant lake. For a moment her new husband didn't hear her soft footsteps on the grass—he was far too engrossed in staring intently at the baby. It gave her just long enough for her stupid heart to turn over with longing at the vision they made, and then to collect herself before he noticed her reaction.

A huge, coach-built pram which had been sent down from Rome was parked beside an arbour which was spilling over with flowers. Soft, creamy-pink flowers with such an intoxicating fragrance which seemed to perfume the whole garden, and Aisling breathed in their scent as if her senses had been starved.

Gianluca was still in his dark wedding suit but he had

removed his tie as he always did at the first opportunity—and had undone a couple of shirt buttons. He looked up from where he had been leaning over the pram, and Aisling suddenly felt almost weak with longing.

Gianluca stared at her with a thudding kind of disappointment and disbelief because it was as though the woman he had married today had gone through some sort of transformation. Like Cinderella in reverse, he thought bitterly. Gone was the sexy bride in her vertiginous shoes and the demure yet sexy ivory silk dress. In their place were some dull-looking trousers and an equally dull-looking shirt.

Well, what had he expected? He had forced her hand into matrimony and perhaps she had now decided it was time to flex her own muscles. To punish him. As a message of how she intended to conduct this marriage, it could not have been clearer.

'You've changed,' he observed softly.

Aisling was suddenly aware of a new hardness in his eyes. 'The dressing-up part of the day is over, Gianluca—and, besides, this is much easier for feeding Claudio.' She peered over at the pram rather desperately. 'How is he?'

'He's asleep,' he said abruptly.

'Oh. Well, that's…good.' Aisling stood there, feeling—redundant. She couldn't even pick the baby up because if she did that she might look selfish—as if she was using him as some sort of prop, because she wasn't sure what to do with *herself*.

'So tell me—what do you want to do tonight? This our wedding night,' he mocked.

She stared at him nervously, unsure of what to say. 'Do you have any suggestions?'

'You mean, other than the very obvious ones a groom might make to his new bride on such an occasion?' His black eyes glittered. 'I think you know the answer to that question, *cara*. And while you think about it, you will excuse me—for I have a few calls I need to make.'

Aisling stared at him in dismay. 'But I thought you were taking a break for your honeymoon!'

'I'm here, aren't I?' he drawled insolently. 'You have some ideas, perhaps? You want to drink a little champagne, or call on the chef and have him prepare us a few things to nibble on? Curl up together and watch a movie?'

'Please don't be sarcastic, Gianluca.'

'Maybe I damned well *feel* like being sarcastic!' he retorted hotly.

One of them needed to confront it and it looked as if it was going to have to be her. 'About the sleeping arrangements.' Help me out, her eyes appealed to him—but his handsome face remained faintly quizzical, as if he had nothing to do with the decision. She hesitated, unsure of how best to put it. Just tell him. Tell him you're willing to share his bed tonight.

Gianluca almost laughed aloud at her pale face and the wary expression in her cool eyes. Did she think that he was going to start exercising his conjugal rights? To go over to her and take her in his arms and to kiss that sour little expression off her face until he was inside her?

Instead, his mouth flattened. 'Oh, do not worry, *cara*. I am not so desperate for your body that I need to come begging you to take me into your bed. If I find that desire overwhelms me, then there are plenty of women who would relish the experience—rather than seeking it from one for whom the notion is so obviously abhorrent.'

'Abhorrent?' she echoed, bewildered. 'Where the hell did you get that idea from?'

'Your face tells its own story,' he said softly.

Even if he didn't have a clue about her true feelings for him, surely he must have realised that she was nervous—as any woman would have been in these extraordinary circumstances? 'I'm apprehensive,' she admitted carefully.

Of what? he wondered. Of letting that icy composure slip? She seemed determined to keep him at an emotional arm's length—and he could cope with that. But if they put physical distance between them, then this whole situation would quickly become intolerable, and surely Aisling was intelligent enough to realise that.

Gianluca's eyes narrowed. She operated like a man in the way she compartmentalised her life. So why not present his proposition in a way she would find acceptable?

He moved towards her and lifted his hand to her face, slowly and thoughtfully using it to sculpt the shape of her chin, allowing the pad of his thumb to briefly graze across the lips which trembled. He observed the darkening of her eyes as he drew his hand away.

'I want you,' he said starkly.

'Gianluca—'

'I shall come to you tonight,' he said softly. 'And if you want me, then you must leave your door open. That is your choice. If it is shut, I shall not come to you again.'

Oh, *why* didn't he seal his intent with a kiss? she wondered desperately. Why talk about it in those hard, cold terms as if it was some kind of takeover bid? Because that was *exactly* what it was. First her baby, and now her body—of *course* he wanted them both.

But Aisling wasn't stupid. She wanted him, too—with a fierce hunger which frightened her. A need which was born out of the heart as much as the body. She was afraid of where all this was going to lead—but she forced her mind to draw back from the dark, torturous routes of her imagination.

Why project into an unknown future? She might get hurt, yes—but she suspected she was going to get hurt anyway and only a fool would deny herself as much pleasure as possible in the meantime.

But there was no need to be a walkover. Keep him guessing. In the past she had given in to him all too easily—surely the only way to keep his interest alive was to not be a sure bet? Hadn't he once told her that himself—that the thing about her which appealed to him was the fact that she was so enigmatic?

'I'll give it some thought,' she said coolly.

Oh, but she was awesome, he thought—with reluctant admiration. Like a cold and brilliant diamond. He gave a soft laugh. 'Just one more thing, Aisling.'

She swallowed, her heart beating so fast that she could barely get the word out. 'What?'

His eyes flickered to the tight pony tail. 'If I come to you tonight,' he said softly, 'be sure to let down your hair.'

CHAPTER TWELVE

'I GUESS you must be thinking about going back to work,' said Gianluca abruptly.

'Work?' echoed Aisling blankly as she looked up from spooning some mashed banana into Claudio's sweet little mouth. She dabbed the edges of its rosebud shape with a napkin, and smiled lovingly at her baby. Feeding him always took longer than she thought it would—in fact, everything seemed to take longer. Why did no one tell you that having a baby could be such an absorbing and time-consuming job?

And it wasn't just the feed itself which took time, but the fact that she seemed to want to study Claudio intently to see whether he might have grown an extra centimetre overnight.

And when she wasn't studying him, she found herself just as tempted by a sneaky scrutiny of his father. Did Gianluca have any idea of just how sexy he looked when he was fresh out of the shower and had just thrown on an old pair of jeans and a sweater? she thought longingly. Save it until later, she told herself. Until you're in bed. Don't give yourself away with your wistful yearnings.

At least in bed she didn't have to pretend—because she

had discovered that sex had other kinds of uses than pleasure. She could use it to air all those emotions she usually kept hidden away. In bed, she could dare to love him with her lips and her body—even if she dared not use the words he had no requirement for.

'Yes, work,' said Gianluca, in an impatient kind of voice. He subjected her to a cool, questioning scrutiny. 'You were adamant about continuing your career when you agreed to come out to Italy, weren't you, Aisling? As I recall, it was your number one worry—'

'I wouldn't have said it was my number one—'

'Perhaps not,' said Gianluca, overriding her objection as if she hadn't spoken. He could see her frown of confusion—but what the hell did she expect? That he hadn't noticed the way she behaved? Spending her days like some kind of efficient robot and only coming to flesh-and-blood life in his arms at night? She might try to disguise her dissatisfaction with her life here, but he could sense her edginess—that wary way she had of looking at him sometimes. He could not deny that she had thrown herself wholeheartedly into motherhood, but anyone could see that there was something lacking in her life. He narrowed his eyes. 'I take it you *do* want to go back?'

Had he noticed her e-mailing Suzy to get all the latest updates, then? Aisling wondered. Or scouring the financial pages of the international newspapers she had requested because she was terrified of being left behind—of being properly isolated in every sense of the word? Or had he just tapped into her own insecurity—that with her immersion into motherhood she was becoming so unlike the person she had been that she didn't even recognise *herself*, these days.

And that was *dangerous*. Because a world dominated by an undemonstrative husband in this lazily beautiful setting was lulling her into a false sense of security—and surely her career was her ticket to freedom if it all went disastrously wrong. If she relied on Gianluca to be the kind of husband she longed for him to be—waiting for some change of heart which would never come—then she risked losing everything she had ever worked for. Just like her mother.

Wasn't work her one solid island in a swirling sea of uncertainty? Something she could rely on when everything else around her seemed so temporary. Even the peace she experienced in this heavenly idyll of a place seemed fragile, as if reality might shatter it at any moment.

Yes, she felt cosseted and protected by Gianluca—but only in a superficial and very physical sense. As if he would move heaven and earth to ensure the comfort of the woman who had borne his child. But emotionally, there was nothing. He was remote. Watchful. Restrained.

And *he* was working again, wasn't he? Sometimes from home, true—but more often than not driving into his offices in Rome. He was mixing in the glossy world of business and takeovers, while she was changing into a dull little housewife who surely he would find increasingly less attractive?

'Of course I want to go back to work,' she said quietly.

Gianluca poured himself a cup of coffee. Should he have been surprised at her agreement? Disappointed, maybe? His mouth hardened. Of course not. Circumstances might have changed, but Aisling had not—and underneath it all she was still the ice-cool, ambitious businesswoman she always had been.

'So we might as well hire a nanny, mightn't we?' he said smoothly, dropping a cube of sugar into his cup

'N-nanny?' she echoed.

He gave her an unfathomable look. '*Sì, cara.* With two working parents, there's no other solution, is there?' And he bent his head and began to read the business section of his newspaper.

Aisling stared at his dark head, feeling as if she'd just been wrong-footed—like a defendant in court who had just been tripped up by the prosecution. How tense he seemed this morning. Almost as if he *wanted* to pick a fight with her. 'Gianluca,' she questioned hesitantly. 'Is something *wrong*?'

His smile was bland as he looked up at her. 'Why should anything be wrong, *cara*? We have a healthy baby and have proved we can exist in relative harmony for most of the time. You have met many of my friends and you all seem to like one another. We argue intelligently about politics and films, there are enough staff here to ensure that life runs smoothly—and at night you become a sensual witch in my arms.' And it felt like living in a damned *vacuum*. He raised his eyebrows in question. 'What more could a man ask for?'

The undercurrent and the tension in the air were almost palpable. Aisling felt as if he were asking her some kind of trick question which she had no idea how to answer. 'We'll advertise for a nanny, then,' she said stiffly. 'That should help.'

They interviewed the prospective candidates together, even though Aisling would have preferred to vet them all by herself.

'Isn't this more my territory than yours?' she asked him lightly. 'Do you really want to be bothered with all this?'

'Haven't you seen those horror films where the nanny turns out to be a psycho?' he queried acidly. 'I'd rather have some say in the matter, if you don't mind.'

She knew that made sense, since whoever they chose would inevitably be Italian and Aisling's command of the language was very basic indeed. Nonetheless, she shocked herself by wanting to bin all the applications from any attractive woman under thirty. Correction. *Any* woman she thought might be eying up Gianluca—because there was a stunning widow of forty she found rather threatening.

Was she going to become one of those chronically insecure women who was always terrified that her husband was going to have affairs with other women? And would that be such an unreasonable fear, under the circumstances?

'Perhaps you could explain your criteria for rejecting some of these perfectly good candidates?' questioned Gianluca sardonically.

'They just have to *feel* right,' said Aisling stubbornly, thinking that if one more applicant slanted him a look from beneath her eyelashes, she would scream out loud. 'It's a woman thing.'

In the end they both agreed on Carmela, who was just twenty and sweetly serious. But she was the one who seemed most captivated by Claudio—though bizarrely Aisling found herself wanting her not to get *too* attached to her baby.

And she quickly discovered that having a nanny was different from having all the other people who worked in and around the vast estate for Gianluca. They tended to get on with their jobs and fade into the background, but a nanny was a fairly constant presence and Aisling found it inhibiting.

Not because she and Gianluca were constantly snatching kisses—they definitely weren't, since all their physical affection never left the bedroom. But it was unsettling having someone else around as an unwitting observer. Or rather, it made her feel unsettled—and start to think that perhaps something *did* need to change. As if seeing the situation through an outsider's eyes made her realise how unsatisfactory it all was.

Aisling went upstairs earlier than usual one evening and was trying on one of her suits when she heard the door open quietly, and then close again. She looked up from where she had been struggling to do up a skirt when she saw Gianluca standing there, watching her.

'Those are your work clothes,' he observed.

She met his eyes in the mirror. 'That's right,' she said evenly.

'You're planning to go back?'

'Suzy says there's a job in Paris coming up and she'd rather I handled it—I've dealt with the people before.' She shrugged. 'And I can speak a bit of French.'

'And were you planning to tell me about it?'

She heard the sharp note of accusation in his voice. 'Oh, Gianluca—of course I was! I thought that was why we employed Carmela. Anyway, nothing's been decided yet.'

'It sounds to me as if the decision has already been made.'

'You don't…mind? If I go back?'

'It is not my place to *mind*, *cara*,' he mocked. 'You never claimed to want to stay at home baking biscuits all day.' His black eyes roved slowly over her, enjoying seeing her struggle with the zip.

She swallowed—the ebony stare making her feel acutely self-conscious. 'The damn thing's too tight!' she complained.

'Your hips are rounder since motherhood,' he murmured. 'Buy a different size.'

Suddenly her inability to do the skirt up seemed to symbolise more than just a few extra pounds gained after childbirth. Where had all the control gone from her life? That feeling of order she used to experience—of knowing where she was in the world? 'Are you trying to make me feel worse?' she questioned.

He walked up behind her and slid his hands round to where they lay on the slight curve of her belly.

'Al contrario,' he murmured, sliding his fingers down to press hard and possessively over the mound of her crotch. 'I am trying to make you feel better.'

'Gianluca,' she breathed, because this was exquisitely erotic, with his fingers splayed possessively against her. And more erotic still was the fact that he was now sliding the skirt up over her thighs with a little difficulty until he—and she—could see the neat pale blue triangle of her panties reflected back in the mirror.

'What is it?' he whispered, bending his head so that she could feel his warm breath against her neck as he watched their reflection. He rubbed his fingertips over the triangle experimentally, feeling her squirm and watching her squirm, too.

'I…nothing.' She swallowed as his fingers moved with their own particular rhythm. It seemed too…too *intimate*…

not just to feel him, but to watch him doing it. But then Gianluca seemed to delight in experimentation—to introduce her to wild and wonderful new things and to watch the passion explode within her. 'Do you want to go to…bed?' she stumbled.

'No!' he negated harshly. 'I want to see you come. And I want to see *you* watching yourself come.' In heaven's name, it was the only time she showed any real feeling—the only time she really let go!

'Gianluca!' Her legs buckled and she might have fallen had not the hand that was not moving so surely against her panties whipped up to catch her firmly by the waist. And she realised then that he was not going to stop. Not only that, but neither was she. In fact, she was…was… 'Oh!' Her head tipped back, her eyes closed and she began to moan softly as she writhed against him.

He waited until he had felt her spasming cease and then he pushed her to the ground, straddling her as he ripped apart her panties with a single rent and her eyes flew open in question.

'They were brand-new!' she protested.

'Then I will buy you another pair,' he ground out. 'Only next time I'm going to choose them for you. Something a little more…*ah*…' He shook his head distractedly. 'Aisling! What is it that you do to me? *Impazzire o fare i matti!*' She was driving him crazy. Crazy.

Her eyes were ice and fire now—just as she was—her coolness repelling him as much as exciting him. He was able to possess her, but only in the purely physical sense. He watched the thick lashes flutter down as he drove deep inside her and then before he knew it he was welcoming the warm sweetness of his release—knowing that it would free him from her sensual spell. And, damn it—he *wanted* to be free from it!

They lay there on the floor, still entwined, their clothing in disarray, and Gianluca began to drift off, his hand absently smoothing down her hair as his breathing grew steadier and deeper, and Aisling's heart felt as if it were going to shatter into a million pieces.

He did that tender stroking stuff after making love because that was what he had been conditioned to do, by nature—just as his hard body now required sleep in order to regain its strength.

In this moment, she had everything and yet she had nothing. All she had ever wanted and yet it felt completely empty. Just the same old one-sided relationship it had always been. She might as well have been back where she started—loving him from afar without daring to let it show.

It didn't seem to matter if you made a baby between you and got married as a consequence of that—it didn't change the fundamental facts. And those were that Gianluca simply didn't feel the same way about her. That this life was a kind of compromise—and couldn't she just accept that?

Because what was the alternative?

Aisling stared up at the ceiling, aware of the slow, steady breathing of the man beside her. Maybe she needed to initiate some kind of change—before she went mad with wanting what she could never have. Or worrying that one day he might find it with someone else.

She shook him gently by the shoulder, her fingers caressing the silk of his skin. 'Gianluca,' she said. 'I want to go back to work as soon as possible.'

* * *

'It's only a little trip,' Aisling said as she handed Claudio over to Carmela, and planted yet another kiss on top of his silky black hair. 'And Paris isn't far away.'

'So you come back later today?' asked the Italian girl quietly.

'Well, I'll probably stay overnight because I expect the meeting will run on into dinner.' Aisling saw Gianluca come out of his study, carrying a sheath of papers which looked suspiciously like a contract, and raise his eyebrows at her in question. 'I'll catch a flight back first thing.' She stared at her husband, looking so handsome and yet so impossibly forbidding. 'If that's okay?'

'I think we might just be able to cope without you.' He shot her a mocking black glance. 'Tell me, *cara*, haven't I seen that suit somewhere before?'

Aisling blushed. It was the one she had been trying on. The one…

She had managed to squeeze into it and had expressed enough breast milk for Claudio to be given in her absence, along with a long list of instructions for Carmela about what to do if he wouldn't settle—and for her or Gianluca to ring her immediately if anything went wrong.

But there was no phone call—and while she was pleased that they hadn't *had* to call her, she found herself feeling strangely disappointed, too. Was she so expendable, then? Didn't Gianluca think that she might like to hear an account of the baby's day while she was in a different country—or didn't he care? Silly Aisling. Of course he didn't.

She arrived to a chilly Paris and found it hard to settle during her meetings. Worse, she had little appetite for the delicious restaurant lunch she was taken to in the *arts et metiers* district. In fact, all she wanted to do was to whip out little photos of Claudio and show them round.

Was he missing her? she wondered. Was he doing that little thing he did when he'd just been fed—of lying on his back and kicking his darling little feet in the air? Gianluca always said one day he would become a striker for one of the top Italian clubs—while she had argued that he would be much better playing for an English side. Until they'd both decided that maybe football was a risky career for such a talented child.

But thinking like that didn't help matters. It made her imagine an unimaginable future and ache with an odd kind of emptiness.

Stupidly, she found herself wishing she were back in her beautiful house with her beautiful baby—watching her beautiful man. Suddenly, she remembered how gentle *Il Tigre* could be. A strong man who could cradle a baby with infinite tenderness. Her heart turned over.

What wouldn't she give for Gianluca to be missing her, too?

By mid-afternoon, she still hadn't heard from them and she rang the house, but there was no answer. She tried Gianluca's phone, but it just went straight through to voice-mail and she left several messages asking him to call.

By late afternoon, she was frantic. Frantic enough to cut short her meeting and to cancel dinner and her hotel room and catch an early flight back to Perugia.

An empty stomach and self-doubt made her imagination work overtime. Claudio was sick. Gianluca had taken this opportunity to have the locks changed so she couldn't get in! Gianluca had gone off with another woman! She had neglected her child by zooming off to the French capital and he would make her pay. And even though the rational side of her brain told her that these were crazy thoughts without foundation—that didn't make them seem any less real.

She had to switch her phone off during the flight, but by the time they landed and she switched it back on again a text had come through from Gianluca saying, rather cryptically: 'We're fine—what's the panic?'

But by then Aisling was being fuelled by adrenaline and at the airport she leapt into a taxi with her nerves in shreds, knowing she couldn't go on like this. That she was living her life the wrong way and sooner or later it would drive her insane.

Yet even as these thoughts were racing through her head she was aware that she was plotting like a master-criminal, knowing that she wanted to arrive at the house early and unannounced. To surprise Gianluca. To find him doing...*what*?

The taxi crunched its way up the hillside and Aisling had it stop outside the main entrance. Thrusting a note into the driver's hand, she slipped in through a side gate and went running inside, throwing open the door with a shaking hand, but there was nobody to be seen in the vast hallway.

'Hello?' she called, and then again as she closed the door behind her, only this time louder. 'Hel-*lo*!'

There was nothing but the ominous sound of silence and a cold, sick feeling clamped round her stomach until she heard the distant sound of a sonorous voice coming from upstairs—and she took the stairs two at a time, heading for the direction of the voice, which seemed to be coming from the nursery bathroom.

She burst into the room with all the urgency of a firefighter and then halted in her tracks to see the vision which greeted her.

Gianluca was on the floor with the sleeves of his shirt all rolled up, tickling the tummy of a newly bathed Claudio, who was lying on a big, fluffy dry towel beside him. He'd dressed the baby in a new Babygro festooned with blue bunnies, which Aisling had bought in Rome only last week, and Claudio was gurgling with delight at the attention. They both turned their heads at the sound of the door and Aisling stood there, blinking back stupid tears of shame and remorse.

How *could* she have thought that Gianluca might have been up to no good—when he was all splashed with water and laughing at his son and looking like a leading contender for a Father of the Year award?

'Gianluca,' she said, her voice shaking with emotion as he sat back on his heels, his black eyes narrowing with an expression she couldn't quite work out.

This, he thought, was Aisling as he had rarely seen her. Her hair was falling out untidily all over her shoulders, her tights had a run in them and her face was pink and shiny, as if she'd been sprinting. But the difference was about more than her dishevelled physical appearance. He could see her face working, like someone who was trying very hard not to cry. Aisling *crying*? Surely not. 'You're early,' he observed.

'Where *were* you?'

His eyes hardened. 'Do I have to give an account of my movements every time you're away?'

'I couldn't get through all day and I was *worried*!'

'About what?' He gave a short laugh. 'Presumably not

about leaving your son with his father or with the nanny whom *you* helped vet? So what's to be worried about, Aisling? Maybe you just couldn't bear the thought of losing control—of the world functioning perfectly well without you always being in the driving seat. Isn't that closer to the truth?'

She stared at him. She had been tightly gripping onto her handbag, but now it slid unnoticed from her fingers as she registered his caustic tone. What sort of monster was he describing? 'What are you saying?' she whispered.

He shook his head. 'Not now, Aisling,' he said harshly. 'And not in front of the baby. If there has to be some kind of showdown, then let's do it by upsetting as few people as possible.'

Showdown?

Aisling felt dizzy as he picked up Claudio and carried him into the nursery. 'Where's Carmela?' she questioned breathlessly as she followed him.

'I gave her the evening off.' He turned his head and she could see the mirthless line of his mouth. 'Or maybe should I have run that past you first?'

Aisling stared at him and a slow, steady thump of fear began to work her heart into a different beat. She had been planning to tell him that she thought things needed to change, but now it looked as if Gianluca had come to a similar sort of conclusion himself and suddenly she was scared.

'Can I put him to bed? I haven't seen him all day.'

'Of course.' He kissed Claudio's head and handed him over—barely meeting her eyes.

'I'd better feed him, too.'

He was going to say that Claudio had taken most of the

bottle she'd left behind, but by then she was already lifting her shirt with trembling fingers and latching the baby to her. Was she doing that to emphasise the fact that the baby needed a mother in the way that it never could need its father? He heard Claudio's little sound of contentment and then the glugging of him feeding and saw Aisling briefly close her eyes with relief.

And, God forgive him, but at that moment he felt excluded. An outsider. Hadn't he seen articles about fathers sometimes feeling jealous of their babies and hadn't he despised them? Yet now here he was, feeling something very close to envy. He turned his back on her with a gesture of finality. 'I'll be waiting for you downstairs,' he said.

Had he meant that to sound like a threat? Aisling forced herself to relax while Claudio fed, but it felt as if a soft dark cloud of dread were waiting to descend on her shoulders. It should have been a glorious homecoming—her baby safe and happy—with a sense of achievement that she'd managed to do a day's work. Except that she hadn't, had she—not really?

The whole day had been a disaster from start to finish. She hadn't been able to concentrate on her work properly and yet she hadn't been there for Claudio either, and now Gianluca was waiting for her downstairs with a strange and sombre look on his face and she was terrified of what that might mean.

That life was better when she wasn't around—and now that Claudio was entrenched in this rural paradise she would have the devil's job ever prising him away from it.

She spent longer than she needed to cuddling her little boy and then putting him down in the cot. As if she was trying to hold onto these last few moments of innocence before her world was shattered in a way which instinct told her it was about to be.

Flicking the mobile which hung over the crib with her fingertip, Aisling watched the tiger spinning round and round, its distinctive gold and black colouring blurring into something unrecognisable and indistinct—just as her life seemed to have done since meeting Gianluca.

Was it over? she wondered as she switched on the night-light and slowly made her way downstairs.

Probably. And maybe it would be better like that—with all this need for pretence gone. She used to think she had everything mapped out, rigidly put in its place. She had thought that if you hid how you were really feeling, then you wouldn't get hurt. But she had been wrong—because she had opened up the way for the kind of hurt which was a million times worse than anything else she'd ever experienced before.

She had grown up under a canopy of fear—and that had carried on into her adult life. But fear didn't make a situation better—it made it worse. Fear that Gianluca might one day leave her or slowly edge her from his life was spoiling what time they had together now.

He was waiting for her in the smallest of the reception rooms with only a couple of low-lamps on and a fire which had been lit against the newly chilly evenings. Flames danced shadows over the walls and ceiling, and she could hear the crackle and spit of the logs.

He'd opened wine, too—she could see that it was a bottle from his own estate with its distinctive Palladio label—and he had poured two glasses. Viewed from here, it looked like a picture-perfect family scene. The husband and the wife who had just put their adorable baby to bed. The glow of the room and the pleasurable anticipation of the evening ahead. Suddenly, Aisling felt weak. She wanted to freeze-frame it and keep it, but it wasn't real, and yet the pain in her heart had become so very real.

Gianluca saw her face whiten and his eyes narrowed. 'What's happened?' he demanded. 'Is something wrong?'

She hesitated. What would she usually say? *No, I'm fine—just a little tired, that's all.* She wouldn't want him to think she was less than perfect—because Gianluca wanted and expected perfection. But she wasn't—and her elaborately constructed act wasn't working anyway.

'Yes, something is wrong,' she said, slumping into the nearest chair and beginning to cry. 'Something is very wrong. You know it is!'

Gianluca watched her. Usually, he mistrusted a woman's tears—for they were often used as tools of manipulation—but these were sliding down her pale cheeks and her mouth was twisting in pain. And this was *Aisling*, he reminded himself. She always hid her emotions and she was not a manipulator. She never cried.

His cool expression did not change as he sipped his drink. 'A hitch at work, perhaps?'

Aisling flinched as if he had struck her—but then, in a way, hadn't he done just that? Because a crushing emotional blow could wound just as savagely. 'Is that how you see me, then?' she questioned, her voice shaking. 'As so driven and focussed that nothing but ambition can touch me?'

'I thought that was how you saw yourself.'

'If you knew how I saw myself—you'd run a million

miles away, Gianluca.' She lowered her voice, daring to voice her deepest fear—bringing it out from the dark cupboard of her imagination. 'But perhaps you're intending to do that anyway.'

The cord of tension which had been stretching tight within him suddenly snapped as he saw this cold wasteland of a life spread out before him with this clever, closed woman. '*Sì*, maybe I am,' he ground out. 'Because I think I would find anything tolerable to living with a damned mannequin!'

The awful confirmation that he was thinking of leaving her was momentarily eclipsed by his accusation. 'A mannequin?' she echoed in confusion. 'What are you talking about?'

'I am talking about a woman who might as well be made of wax—for all that she lives and breathes. For that is you!' he declared. 'A cool, controlled woman who never shows her feelings—except in bed! You think that I wish to be married to a block of ice?'

She clapped her hand over her heart, it was beating so hard. 'But th-that's what you wanted!'

His eyes narrowed. 'What are you talking about?'

'You told me that's what you found so attractive about me—that you never knew what was going on in my head. That I was an enigma and that men liked a woman to be mysterious—especially a man like you, who had spent all their lives being pursued by women who were like open books!'

He slammed his glass down so hard that some of the wine slopped onto the mantelpiece. 'Yes, that was what initially intrigued me—but certainly not all. Are you crazy—thinking that I would tie my life to a woman simply because she played hard to get? You do not think that I was attracted to your mind as well as your initial reserve?' he questioned hotly, shaking his dark head.

'And we have moved on since then,' he continued furiously. 'Or, rather, I was hoping we might have done. But it seems I have been wrong, my *freddo bella*. What am I supposed to think—if not that what I see is what I get? A woman who does not care for her man? A woman who does not know how to care?'

'But why should that bother you, Gianluca?' she questioned, her voice wobbling. 'You really only ever married me because of the baby, didn't you? Why, you'd never even have seen me again if I hadn't been pregnant!'

'But that was *your* choice, too, Aisling—remember? I don't remember you longing to want to see *me*!' He took a deep breath to control himself, but rarely had he been so on the brink of losing it. 'Yes, the baby was the reason we married, but even if you *did* have my baby—do you really think I would have set up home with a woman if I found her boring? If I did not think there were areas of compatibility we could work on?'

She stared at him. 'You mean, you think there are?'

His breath was coming in short, angry bursts and his eyes burned like hot coals. 'Ah, Aisling—you drive the dagger so deep, don't you? You think that I am responsible for everything, *sì*? You want only to shift the blame to me, so that you do not have to accept any responsibility yourself? Yet you ran from my bed that first night in Italy—when there was no reason for you to do so. You, the only woman I had taken there—and, yes, I admit it was probably because you *were* so damned enigmatic!'

Aisling blinked at him in sheer surprise. 'I didn't know that. And besides, I...*panicked*—'

He gave an impatient wave of his hand. 'Then, when I came to find you in London again—'

'But you kept me waiting for weeks! You told me you were only there because you had business in London!'

'You think I have no pride, *cara*—is that it?' he demanded. 'You think I will allow a woman to trample on my heart? So I took you to dinner and I took you to bed—but again, you could not wait to get away the next morning.'

'But our pact—'

'Pact be damned!' he raged. 'You make me feel like the stud! The gigolo!'

'That was the last thing I intended!' she protested.

He shook his dark head frustratedly, aware that his smooth fluency seemed to be deserting him—but then, he was not used to doing something as alien as articulating his feelings. 'So we have the baby and we make the marriage. We live in the beautiful house and everything should be wonderful. I even agree that you should work if you wish to—because I know how important it is to you! Because I admire the way you have worked your way up from nothing to achieve everything that you have. I encourage you to go to Paris, because I think that is what you want—what you need to make you contented. If work is so important to you, then you should work—but it must be your choice and yours alone. I try to work out what makes you tick—because you refuse to tell me!'

'Gianluca—'

'But even that was not right,' he raged as he cut through her protest with an impatient wave of his hand. 'Because

I was not plaguing you with phone calls all day, leaving you free to concentrate on your job—you are still not happy!'

'I felt excluded,' she whispered. 'As if you wanted to get me out of the way and sideline me.'

He shook his head with something approaching despair. 'Ah, Aisling?' he asked softly. 'Why has it all gone so wrong, *mia cara*?'

Aisling's heart stilled and her breath caught in her throat, knowing that she was poised on an emotional tightrope. It was one of those moments where there was a chance—just a tiny one, but a chance all the same—of pulling back from the brink of disaster. Of retrieving something golden and precious from the mess they had made of it so far.

'Because I'm scared,' she admitted.

His eyes narrowed. 'Scared of what?'

Of so many things—would it repel him if she told him? Would the cool image he had painted of her crumble before his eyes? And even if it did—oughtn't she to take that risk? For she had discovered that a relationship could not be built on shaky foundations—and surely honesty, however painful, was the most secure basis of all.

'Scared of being needy, like my mother. Scared of relying on a man and being left. Scared of not having a career to fall back on if that should happen.'

'But you are *not* your mother!' he objected quietly. 'And I am not your father. Whatever happens, I would not leave you destitute.'

'No. Of course not. I can see that now. But patterns of thinking are hard to break when they've been in you for a lifetime.' She tried a smile but it felt more like a grimace. 'You see the cool stuff is just all a show, Gianluca—a mask

I wear to conceal the ugly insecurities underneath. To hide so many things.' She drew a deep breath now, recognising that she had come so far and she could not back down. That honesty meant just that. Had she really trampled on his heart, as he had claimed? Had she been so busy looking at the popular image of the rich playboy that she had not realised that *he* might be wearing a mask himself?

'Including the fact that I love you,' she declared softly. 'Deep down, I think I've always loved you—but I've done such a good job of hiding it that I don't think you're ever going to believe me.'

As she spoke, as emotion trembled her voice and softened her features, the mask of which she had spoken seemed to dissolve before his eyes.

Suddenly Gianluca could see what it must have cost her to have admitted that and he could also see what had been left behind in its place—a look of tenderness and passion, devotion and love—shining out brighter than any star viewed from a rooftop restaurant. And it melted his heart.

When he had heard she was pregnant, Gianluca had marvelled at how quickly life could change. That it could be transformed in a heartbeat—by life, by death and by love. Everyone knew that deep down, but most people chose to ignore it. They carried on with their lives, blinkered and unseeing. It was easy to forget that the important things were all around if only you had the courage to reach out for them.

Something had happened when he had first held his newborn son and Gianluca was experiencing something similar now. It *was* love. Like something which had always been just around the corner and out of sight—only now it had stepped out into the daylight at last, dazzling and transforming.

And along with the breathtaking leap of his heart came the feeling of liberation. That just as Aisling had opened up her heart to him—he was free to do the same. Having Claudio had taught him that expressing emotion did not make a man weak—indeed, that love could empower you with a strength which made you feel you could conquer the world.

Gianluca had been protective of his emotions because women had always wanted more from him than he had been prepared to give, but for the first time in his life he had met someone who had not pushed him for emotional commitment or declaration. And love given freely was so much more powerful than love which was demanded.

He felt infused with the same kind of power which could make an eagle soar over unimaginable heights. 'You may not believe me when I tell you that I love you, Aisling,' he said fiercely. 'But believe me when I tell you this, *mia bella…bella*—that I will spend the rest of my life showing you just how much I do.'

Afterwards, Aisling couldn't remember which of them had moved first—whether he had crossed the room or she had. Or maybe it had just happened like osmosis—one flowing into the other without really trying. Just two people with aching hearts who had found a healing remedy in each other.

EPILOGUE

'SO WHAT'S it like working with your wife, Signor Palladio?'

Gianluca smiled at the reporter. 'I've worked with her before. It's how we met.' And then he shook his head to negate any more questions before climbing into the back of the limousine beside Aisling.

The car gathered speed and she snuggled in next to him. To huge international fanfare, they had signed on the Vinoly hotel that very morning and were now going home to the vineyard, to where Claudio was waiting for them.

'I can't wait to see him,' Aisling murmured.

He smiled. 'Me, neither.'

'Though I feel a little guilty sometimes, *caro*,' she admitted softly. 'For leaving my child.'

'All women seem to feel that guilt,' Gianluca observed thoughtfully as he traced his finger around the sensual curves of her lips. 'But you work such limited hours—it's a perfect arrangement.'

It was indeed. Secure in Gianluca's love, Aisling had been able to make the decision about what her working future would entail, and it had been deliciously easy. She wanted her family—her precious little family—to be the number one priority.

So she had sold her share of the business to Suzy—and acted as Gianluca's part-time Human Resource Consultant in Italy. It suited them all very well—though the press found it endlessly fascinating that such a famous bachelor should have embraced such a close partnership with his wife, and with such enthusiasm.

Aisling adored her new life—with her darling Gianluca and adorable baby. Sometimes she woke up in the morning feeling as though she were still in a wonderful dream of living in the soft, Umbrian countryside and experiencing its simple values and community closeness. But she and her successful husband were able to pick up their metropolitan existence any time they liked.

In order to appease all their disappointed friends who hadn't been invited to the wedding, they were throwing a huge house-party at the vineyard this weekend and people were flying in for it from all over the world.

'Just find us a hunk like Gianluca!' Suzy and Ginger had begged.

'I'll try,' Aisling had promised, laughing—knowing deep down that there was no other man in the world who could hold a candle to him.

Gianluca was watching her as the fields passed by in an emerald blur. 'Happy?' he murmured.

'Blissfully.' She turned to him as he began to unclip her hair with that look of sexy intent which had her stomach dissolving with anticipation.

'So, why,' she giggled as it began to spill down over her smart work-suit in a way which made her feel quite decadent—which was exactly what he intended her to feel, 'wouldn't you let me cut it when I wanted to?'

'Because…' Gianluca lifted a long dark strand of hair away from her face and wound it round and round his hand so that it brought her face right up close to his and she could feel the warmth of his breath. 'Because your long hair was always the one factor which defied your practical nature, and I've decided that I would miss it, *cara*.'

'But…but I thought you hated the chignon!' she protested breathlessly.

'No.' He began to drift his lips across the silk satin of her mouth. 'I just didn't like what it represented. Little Miss Uptight. Now I enjoy the contrast of your different looks.' And these days she presented him with so many that he was spoilt for choice.

His own Aisling. *Cara bella.*

Wife. Mother. Soul mate.

* * * * *

Look for LAST WOLF WATCHING
by Rhyannon Byrd—the exciting conclusion in the
BLOODRUNNERS *miniseries*
from Silhouette Nocturne.

Follow Michaela and Brody on their fierce journey to find the truth and face the demons from the past, as they reach the heart of the battle between the Runners and the rogues.

Here is a sneak preview of book three,
LAST WOLF WATCHING.

Michaela squinted, struggling to see through the impenetrable darkness. Everyone looked toward the Elders, but she knew Brody Carter still watched her. Michaela could feel the power of his gaze. Its heat. Its strength. And something that felt strangely like anger, though he had no reason to have any emotion toward her. Strangers from different worlds, brought together beneath the heavy silver moon on a night made for hell itself. That was their only connection.

The second she finished that thought, she knew it was a lie. But she couldn't deal with it now. Not tonight. Not when her whole world balanced on the edge of destruction.

Willing her backbone to keep her upright, Michaela Doucet focused on the towering blaze of a roaring bonfire that rose from the far side of the clearing, its orange flames burning with maniacal zeal against the inky black curtain of the night. Many of the Lycans had already shifted into their preternatural shapes, their fur-covered bodies standing like monstrous shadows at the edges of the forest as they waited with restless expectancy for her brother.

Her nineteen-year-old brother, Max, had been attacked by a rogue werewolf—a Lycan who preyed upon humans for food. Max had been bitten in the attack, which meant he was no longer human, but a breed of creature that existed between the two worlds of man and beast, much like the Bloodrunners themselves.

The Elders parted, and two hulking shapes emerged from the trees. In their wolf forms, the Lycans stood over seven feet tall, their legs bent at an odd angle as they stalked forward. They each held a thick chain that had been wound around their inside wrists, the twin lengths leading back into the shadows. The Lycans had taken no more than a few steps when they jerked on the chains, and her brother appeared.

Bound like an animal.

Biting at her trembling lower lip, she glanced left, then right, surprised to see that others had joined her. Now the Bloodrunners and their family and friends stood as a united force against the Silvercrest pack, which had yet to accept the fact that something sinister was eating away at its foundation—something that would rip down the protective walls that separated their world from the humans'. It occurred to Michaela that loyalties were being announced tonight—a separation made between those who would stand with the Runners in their fight against the rogues and those who blindly supported the pack's refusal to face reality. But all she could focus on was her brother. Max looked so hurt…so terrified.

"Leave him alone," she screamed, her soft-soled, black satin slip-ons struggling for purchase in the damp earth as she rushed toward Max, only to find herself lifted off the ground when a hard, heavily muscled arm clamped around her waist from behind, pulling her clear off her feet. "Damn it, let me down!" she snarled, unable to take her eyes off her brother as the golden-eyed Lycan kicked him.

Mindless with heartache and rage, Michaela clawed at the arm holding her, kicking her heels against whatever part of her captor's legs she could reach. "Stop it," a deep, husky voice grunted in her ear. "You're not helping him by losing it. I give you my word he'll survive the ceremony, but you have to keep it together."

"Nooooo!" she screamed, too hysterical to listen to reason. "You're monsters! All of you! Look what you've done to him! How dare you! *How dare you!*"

The arm tightened with a powerful flex of muscle, cinching her waist. Her breath sucked in on a sharp, wailing gasp.

"Shut up before you get both yourself and your brother killed. I will *not* let that happen. Do you understand me?" her captor growled, shaking her so hard that her teeth clicked together. "Do you understand me, Doucet?"

"Damn it," she cried, stricken as she watched one of the guards grab Max by his hair. Around them Lycans huffed and growled as they watched the spectacle, while others outright howled for the show to begin.

"That's enough!" the voice seethed in her ear. "They'll tear you apart before you even reach him, and I'll be damned if I'm going to stand here and watch you die."

Suddenly, through the haze of fear and agony and outrage in her mind, she finally recognized who'd caught her. *Brody.*

He held her in his arms, her body locked against his powerful form, her back to the burning heat of his chest. A low, keening sound of anguish tore through her, and her head dropped forward as hoarse sobs of pain ripped from her throat. "Let me go. I have to help him. *Please*," she begged brokenly, knowing only that she needed to get to Max. "Let me go, Brody."

He muttered something against her hair, his breath warm against her scalp, and Michaela could have sworn it was a single word…. But she must have heard wrong. She was too upset. Too furious. Too terrified. She must be out of her mind.

Because it sounded as if he'd quietly snarled the word *never*.

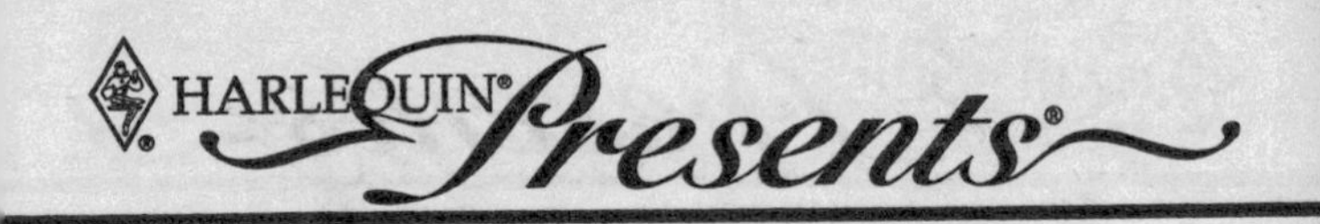
HARLEQUIN® Presents®

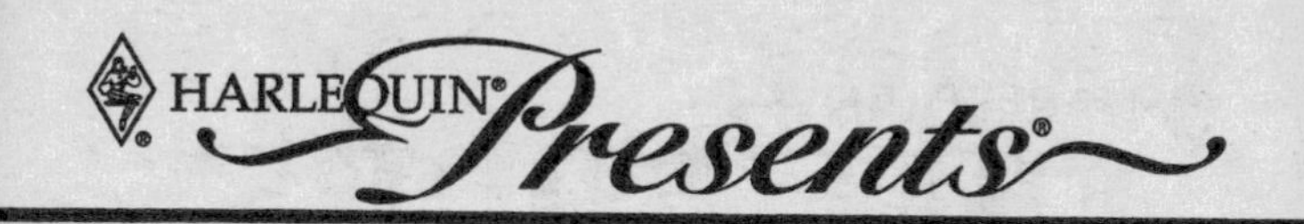

Don't miss favorite author

Michelle Reid's

next book, coming in May 2008,
brought to you only
by Harlequin Presents!

THE MARKONOS BRIDE

#2723

Aristos is bittersweet for Louisa: here, she met and married gorgeous Greek playboy Andreas Markonos and produced a precious son. After tragedy, Louisa was compelled to leave. Five years later, she is back….

Look out for more spectacular stories from Michelle Reid, coming soon in 2008!

HARLEQUIN® Presents®